GLORIOUS THINGS

Barbara Anderson is the author of five novels, *Girls High*, *Portrait of the Artist's Wife* (winner of the 1992 Wattie Award), *All the Nice Girls*, *The House Guest* and *Proud Garments*, and a collection of stories, *I think we should go into the jungle*. She lives in New Zealand.

By the same author

I think we should go into the jungle

Girls High

Portrait of the Artist's Wife

All the Nice Girls

The House Guest

Proud Garments

GLORIOUS THINGS
AND OTHER STORIES

Barbara Anderson

JONATHAN CAPE
LONDON

Published by Jonathan Cape 1999

2 4 6 8 10 9 7 5 3 1

First published in Great Britain in 1999 by
Jonathan Cape
Random House, 20 Vauxhall Bridge Road, London SWlV 2SA

Random House Australia (Pty) Limited
20 Alfred Street, Milsons Point, Sydney,
New South Wales 2061, Australia

Random House New Zealand Limited
18 Poland Road, Glenfield,
Auckland 10, New Zealand

Random House South Africa (Pty) Limited
Endulini, 5A Jubilee Road, Parktown 2193, South Africa

Random House UK Limited Reg. No. 954009

Grateful thanks to the editors of
*Landfall, London Magazine, Metro,
Soho Square, Sport* and *Vital Writing,*
and to Radio New Zealand
and the BBC

Most of these stories were published by
Victoria University Press, New Zealand in 1997
as *The Peacocks and other stories*

A CIP catalogue record for this book
is available from the British Library

ISBN 0-224-05953-X

Printed and bound in Great Britain by
Mackays of Chatham PLC

In Memoriam
Dorothea Turner
1910–1997

Contents

The Westerly

There's not a lot of action round Hils' Haven Motel tonight. Slow, you could call it. Definitely slow. Only a young couple in the left front and a single out the back and two families up the far end of the pool. It would break your heart.

The Reception Area looks onto the road, straight at the corner they crawl round before dropping down to the town, or village more like. I want to leap up from my desk and rush out screaming and waving to stop the cars and the trucks and the buses even. 'Come in,' I'll yell. 'Come in and stay. It's good value. It's clean. We'll make you happy. Come in, for God's sake.'

What'll we do otherwise, Lloyd and me? What'll we do, but I won't tell them that. I won't tell them anything, of course, but I'd like to, it's that frustrating. I see them coming and they slow right down and I'm willing them to turn in beneath the neon and draw up outside and the man to come in. 'Any chance of a week?' he'll say. 'You have! Great. Hear that, love? The lady's got one by the pool.' And all the kids pile out with their baseball caps on backwards and their bright baggy shorts if they're boys and it's summer, and all of them in T-shirts.

1

But then they drive on. Well, they don't because they didn't stop in the first place, but you know what I mean. Lloyd thinks I'm mad. He says I make it worse for myself. Maybe I do, but I can't help hoping.

'What's the point of hoping,' he says. 'If they stop, they stop, right, and if they don't, they drive on.' He doesn't mind really, though. He knows it's because I care. Not only the money, though that too, of course. We put our hearts into Hils' Haven. Both of us.

He insisted on calling the motel after me. Mum christened me Hilary but I was Hils right from a baby and all through Primary. When I got to High I wrote it with a Z for a while, you know how kids mess about with their signatures on assignments and things and I liked the fat tail on the Z. But I went back to S later.

I said to Lloyd when he suggested Hils' Haven, 'I like the name too, but not for a motel. Why not Ace of Spades or El Paradiso or Buena Vista even? Something sort of frisky to show they'll have a nice time. Hils isn't lucky,' I said without thinking.

His face went sad. 'I thought you'd like it.'

'I do like it but it lacks pizzazz.' I'd seen the word in my little weekly in an article about how Hollywood didn't have it any more and the great days were over. I was trying to get away from the unlucky aspect before he thought of the baby too.

That was why we started the motel, because of our little girl, Ilona. She was a dear little thing. I know all mothers say that but you should've seen her. I suppose she was more cute than pretty. She didn't have blonde curls or big blue eyes but when she snuggled up to me, clinging tight as a toy koala on a pencil, I could've died of happiness.

2

It was so sudden how she went. She had diarrhoea and vomiting when she was four and a half and I took her to the doctor and he said she must go straight into hospital because she was dehydrated. I'd never heard of it even. I didn't know that it meant she would be on a drip. The young doctor couldn't get the needle into the vein and I was trying to hold her still and her screaming, I can't tell you what it was like. But he got there in the end and she perked up quite quickly. I sat with her all day and coloured in with her and read a story about chickens, which was her favourite, and stayed while she slept, in case she woke up and was frightened. But at bed-time they said I had to go home. You couldn't stay the night then. I would've slept on the floor or anywhere, but no, they wouldn't have it. So I went home and they rang in the night to say she'd gone. She'd had some sort of collapse. They did a post-mortem. Yes. She had a weakness in the heart, they said.

I've still got her pencil case. I bought it for her because she was that keen to go to school. Kiddies had them months ahead, all ready for when they started. Not plastic fold-over things like nowadays but real cases made of wood and the top half swung out from the bottom and there was a special part hollowed out for the rubber in the top bit. The case was made of some sort of blond wood and had toy soldiers painted on the top with red jackets and those high bearskin hats. That's another thing they probably wouldn't have now – soldiers, especially for a girl. But it was so long ago and they were toy soldiers. She loved it, especially the place for the rubber. I remember the man in the toyshop saying they all like that.

She ran away to school one Saturday morning. We laughed later, but not at the time. Lloyd rushed off in one direction and me in the other and he found her heading through the gate to the local Primary. It was lucky she chose a Saturday. He could show her it was all empty and they came home hand in hand, talking it over. She wanted to learn to read, see, and we didn't know how to teach her.

She was so bright. I met her one day after Playcentre and she said, 'Trucks and lorries are traffic too, you know Mum.' It was the way she came out with it. She'd worked it out after Traffic Drill. I think of that as the trucks change down at the corner. They're traffic too, you know.

But we let her down. Both of us. Not being there when she died. I read a book later about how a mother had insisted on staying with her baby. She said she wasn't going and what were they going to do about it, call the cops? Then she lay down on the floor. Why didn't I do that. Why wasn't I there when she died. Probably nobody was. It was that unexpected.

Bronwyn, the Playcentre lady, said they were going to plant a rose for Ilona and they asked Lloyd and me to be present at the ceremony. So we went. It was kind of them. They were being nice. But when I saw all the kiddies I couldn't stand it. I just couldn't stand it and when Bronwyn handed me the spade, all brand-new and shiny and never used, and asked me to put the last earth around the floribunda, I couldn't and I sobbed, 'No! No! No!' and shoved the spade away. Lloyd picked it up and he finished the job and I clung to him, crying my heart out in front of all the mothers, and the kiddies with their mouths open.

And then Lloyd took me home. I felt I'd let her down again, not planting her rose. But I couldn't. I just couldn't. I haven't seen it since.

We left Hamilton soon after. 'We'll get right away,'

Lloyd said. 'Make a fresh start.' He sold his share of the carrying business to Alan, his partner, and he bought the motel and we came up here to make a fresh start, like he said. I didn't care where we went. But he was right. We had to work so hard, see. There were just the two of us at the beginning and Lloyd kept thinking of new Room Projects, he called them. He'd always been a home handyman, and he had all these ideas he called Hils' Havens. At first I thought who cares, who cares where they sleep if only they can. If I could sleep I wouldn't care if it was in Hils' Haven, or Hils' Hacienda, or Hils' Hangar or wherever.

Lloyd did it all for me, as therapy. For him too of course, but at first all the ideas and everything had to come from him, as well as all the work.

Later I thought up some, like Hils' Hillbilly and Hils' Hideaway for example. In Hideaway the whole unit was done up like a cave. Lloyd did all the structural work required, including a rockface at the back of the bed, but he had to make a bedhead later after a guest flung himself on the bed with a drink, shouting, 'This is the life!' and there was blood everywhere.

We both did the painting and the wallpapering – the whole place was badly run down. I'll never forget how tired I was but it was good being too tired to think. That's why Lloyd insisted.

One of the things of course was finding the wallpapers and all the other things to get the decor right for each unit, but they'd just lifted import restrictions and we had the money from Lloyd's share in the business and there were some lovely things about in Auckland. As well as the rock wall in the Hideaway, we had that wallpaper that looks like rocks, you still see it occasionally in kitchens, and we had those white hairy Greek rugs, they're wilder somehow than sheepskins, and the vanity was hidden by a frill of polished cotton with brown and black cave drawings on it and we had one of those fake-fur covers on the bed. The picture above the bed showed a caveman, or rather lady, cooking over an open fire just outside the cave.

You can see the idea. It was fun to do, working each room out and then getting the decor perfect. We did get a sense of achievement. It saved us at the time. And people loved them.

And now look at it. I can't bear to see them getting run down. For Lloyd's sake especially. And they do need upgrading, there's no denying. The sombrero wallpaper in Hacienda, for instance, and the plastic cactus is shot.

The man had to ping the bell twice. I came to with a jump. He had on pink trousers tucked into flying boots not zipped up, his hair was parted in the middle and he looked angry, his mouth all twisted beneath one of those big moustaches that I think'll date.

She was a washed-out-looking little thing, thin as a wisp with long blonde hair. She wore a plaid jacket over a green cotton frock and jandals. It wasn't a cheerful plaid like a tartan. It was sort of mud-coloured and cream and so big I wondered if it was his. I couldn't imagine a young woman choosing a thing like that, even to keep the wind out, and tonight it was a westerly and hot.

'Got a room?' he said. I've never liked centre partings.

'Yes,' I said, smiling. 'Which one would you like?' I showed him the postcards mounted on the desk of the units we had vacant. It's always been a feature. People like to choose.

'I don't give a stuff,' he said.

I felt as though he'd hit me. Well no, not hit me, but it was a rebuff. I was glad Lloyd wasn't there. He was down town with the truck.

'Could we have Hils' Homely?' she said, pointing. Her smile was nervous, scared almost, as though there wasn't much chance.

It seemed so sad, someone dressed like her wanting to sleep in a cottagey decor, let alone with him. Hils' Homely is my favourite of all. Lloyd isn't so keen. Maybe the treatment isn't so imaginative, like he says, and he didn't have any input into the structure. It's more of a girl's room perhaps. Cottagey. It's all matching, pink and blue flowers on the bedcovers and the curtains, and lots of ruffles and the pillows have white eyelet work. If anyone's booked it I always put a posy on the TV. Pansies, for instance, though of course I hadn't this time, not knowing they were coming.

I gave her a big smile back. She made you feel like that. You had to help her. 'Certainly,' I said. 'Come and I'll show you.' I took the Homely key from its hook and the half-pint of milk from the office fridge, checked the till was locked and came round the desk still smiling.

He strode ahead of us with his behind rolling from one side to the other and she picked up their beat-up green suitcase. He didn't even glance. He knew she'd bring it, that's what got me. You get all sorts, there's no doubt about that. You can't let it worry you, you wouldn't survive otherwise, but I could've kicked him.

You could see straight away that she loved the unit. I

knew she would but it still made me feel good to watch her. She stood just inside the door with her hands clasped to her chest like a skinny little kid. I opened the window. The westerly was more of a gentle breeze round this side and it lifted the ruffled Terylene between the floral drapes. It did look pretty.

I'd spent so much time on this room: the covers, the drapes, even the frill on the stool by the vanity. I'd made them all. 'Do you like it?' I said.

'Yes,' she whispered. 'Oh yes. It's lovely.'

'I'll bring in a wee posy,' I said. 'Just to finish it off. Would you like a few pansies?'

If you'd heard him. 'Not bloody likely,' he roared, laughing and slapping the front of his greasy jeans.

I'm not silly. I knew how he'd taken it, but it was awful.

'I'd love some.' Her voice was that soft I could scarcely hear. She took a step, just one step towards me. I put out my hand and she grabbed it and burst into tears; they were running down her face, splashing like a baby's that can't bear it another minute.

'There, there,' I said. I heard myself saying it. There there.

'Get out,' he muttered, not even looking at me. He kicked his second boot off and turned round. 'And stuff the pansies.'

I went. What could I do.

I told Lloyd when he came back with the truck but he didn't understand. Why should he. What was there to understand.

But I couldn't sleep that night. I couldn't sleep at all and the westerly was there again next morning, blowing grit and sand in through Lloyd's revolving door.

I don't like plastic flowers. I always have fresh on the desk. People remember, usually the ladies of course, but you'd be surprised the number of gentlemen who comment. I always have something in the garden I can pick, even if it's only red photinia leaves. There's always something you can find.

People remember the eggs too. Ever since we opened I've always put one egg per person in the unit fridge. Just the first night, but even so they always ask if they come again. 'Do you still have the eggs?' they say, and I say, 'Of course,' and we laugh. One lady said it was like finding a present from Santa. There's something about eggs, as well as them being unexpected in a motel. Now with the low occupancy I just run round with them later. But last night I hadn't.

I took two out of the office fridge. 'Lloyd,' I said, 'could you pop round to Homely with these?'

'Sure,' he said, and went.

It was the first thing she said next morning. She came into the Reception area and walked straight up to the desk. She was still wearing the same clothes, including that awful jacket, but her smile was beautiful. Shy, like I said, but beautiful. 'The eggs were lovely,' she said.

He was right behind her. 'Come on,' he said, without even a nod at me, and she scurried through the door with him pushing it at her heels. I couldn't tell if it was deliberate – some people never get the hang of revolving doors. But I felt it was, as though it was another way he could get at her.

'Had a nice day?' I said all smiling when they came back,

and then I saw she'd been crying again and he was more angry than ever. I watched his bum jigging from side to side as he headed down the corridor in front of her. Macho. That's what he was. Macho and tough and violent, I shouldn't wonder.

I gripped the Formica tight, I remember that.

She scarcely glanced at me, just ran down the passage after him, her legs knock-kneed and pale above the jandals.

Lloyd took over at the desk at four-thirty. He's good like that. He doesn't leave me stuck there all day and night and anyway there's so much else for me to keep an eye on, like checking on the rooms. We've got a good part-timer called Gerri at the moment but you still have to check. And I pop into the laundry several times a day. You have to. You wouldn't believe the way they leave the irons on, to say nothing of the ones they pinch. I always check the plugholes as well. Nobody else ever deals with the hairs and the gunk and they do block up. So I had my rubber gloves on and my head down when she came in.

'Can I come in?' she said, all quick and nervous.

I jumped. 'Of course, dear,' I said.

She leant against the Bendix. There was a bruise on her cheek. I hadn't noticed it before. 'Can I stay here?' she said.

'Pardon?' I said. I couldn't take my eye off it. It wasn't purple or anything, just a grey smudge under her left eye.

'Stay here,' she said. 'Stay in that room.'

'I don't quite . . .'

'We're leaving tomorrow. He'll be watching me. But I could wait till he's drunk or asleep or something and hitch back. He'd never think of here. Never.'

My head was whirling. 'Stay on in Hils' Homely you mean?'

'Yes, oh yes.' She gasped. One skinny hand was at her mouth; her eyes never left mine. 'Please!'

'But dear . . .'

I had to say it. How could I not say it. Hils' Haven wasn't just mine, it's Lloyd's as well. And the downturn, the endless worry of it all. All that work and effort going down the drain and all the love we put into it as well and both of us trying to pretend there was any point in going on. So I said it.

'Have you any money, dear?'

She shook her head. She didn't say anything. Just shook her head.

We stood there. I pulled off my gloves. I could smell the rubber on my hands as well as the spilt soap powder on the floor and the scorched smell from the ironing board still warm from the last user. And that pinched wee face staring. But even so, even so. I said it.

'No dear,' I said. 'I'm sorry, but no. Things are that bad at the moment. Normally of course we could think of . . .'

She didn't wait. She just gave a sort of yelp and ran out.

When I can't sleep I think of her as well. In the westerly.

We Could Celebrate

Sooze who is my friend, and Bryce who is Sooze's friend, have lent Cliff and me their bach at Paraparaumu for the weekend. They have gone to the wedding of their friend Hester in Te Atatu. Cliff and I watched them as they loaded the car. It made me feel quite faint. All that mountain of stuff in the back is for a one-year-old, their son Jared; reusables, disposables, restrainers, containers, you couldn't see out the back window.

I was pretty thoughtful as they left and Jared waved a bear in a red jacket. So was Cliff. We didn't say anything as we walked back inside.

'Let's go for a swim,' I said, leaping to my feet. I like swimming in the sea. I always start off in my bikini so as not to startle the natives but take off the top and usually the bottom, because I like swimming like that, and in the part where we swim there aren't many people. In the surf you have to hook the straps round your arm then put the same arm through a leg of the bikini so you don't lose them. I did lose a top once but it's worth it for the feel. I don't like sunbathing unless I have a book.

Once, when I was in the Coromandel with an ex-friend of mine called Barry who ditched me, we walked miles and miles up a deserted beach. Right at the end there were three small baches beneath gnarled old pohutukawas in full bloom, it was lovely. But the thing I remember most was an old couple without a stitch on who sat reading in canvas chairs so low their behinds were almost on the paspalum. They were Pakehas but they were tanned mahogany and they just sat there after a quick glance up from their paperbacks and continued reading like a couple of bookish old pelts. I thought that was great and I'd like to have told them so but Barry was getting embarrassed so we walked on. Sometimes I think I'd like to try it but I suppose it only works when you're old, and only then if you've got the sense to play it your way and not fuss.

The shape of her, Christ the shape of her when she swims naked in the sea, leaping over each wave, her nipples hard with the cold, she nearly finishes me. And she has no idea, no vanity, when she's swimming she's swimming, that's what she's there for. She grew up near a good surf beach and still flings herself in front of an unbroken wave like a twelve-year-old, arms clamped to her sides for a good run.

Now I know Carmen, I can believe everything I've ever read or seen about 'the expense of spirit', the fever in the blood; Anthony, the poor wimp with the terrier who abdicated, Othello, the headmistress who killed the diet doctor, any of them. I tell you I could join them, count the world well lost for love and lust and it drives her insane. We have rows about it, flaming dirty gut-wrenching rows because I watch her, want her too much. She calls it eating her. 'Don't eat me, Cliff,' she says, but what can I do. I'm a painter, I look at things, I watch her legs, the angle of the knees as she folds onto the floor, the way she springs

13

upright in one sinuous movement, shall we say. I can't stop
watching her. I sketch her and she's not mad about that so
I have to be quick to catch the angle of her moving arm,
the curve of her bum. Hokusai said any artist should be
able to sketch a man as he fell from a high window to the
ground and I'm getting better. Her arms are the most
beautiful I have ever seen. I watch her plait her hair each
morning. She does it without a mirror, she bends over to
brush it forward, then swings upright, her hands scoop the
pale hair upwards to plait, her fingers move swish swish
and it's done. I've got dozens of her plaiting her hair
because she's concentrating then and doesn't notice me so
much. And of her sleeping. She can sleep on her back, one
hand under her head, her elbow in the air. Try it some
time. Every movement she makes is graceful. Her toes are
prehensile. When she leans her rounded arms over the
back of a chair I am hypnotised and that's just her arms for
God's sake. So what I do, to try and cool things so that I
don't explode and wreck everything, is I clear off quite
often. I get out into the Tararuas with my brother, who
used to be a deer culler and still hunts. I don't shoot but I
like the tracking and Gavin doesn't mind my help in
lugging the stags back through the bush to the car.

And I'm working towards an exhibition, aren't I. Last
week, on the hottest day for three years, I had two free
periods from Girls High, where I teach, and I went round
the galleries to show my stuff. I could feel my feet sweating
in their canvas containers, which didn't help as I ran up the
narrow stairs to the first gallery. The guy was small with a
pink-and-white face and baby hair, and he was wearing
one of those suits that dogs and bears wear in kids'

picturebooks – crumpled and sort of hairy, the colour of Scotch mist. I burst into sweat all over in sympathy but he was cool, very cool and sharp. He didn't say anything as he looked through the portfolio and very little afterwards, except that he'd let me know, and we talked about the art scene in New York and how would I know about that except in magazines and I don't see many of those. I left feeling sick, sick in the gut.

The next owner was a woman. She wore a black beret and it suited her, perched on the back of her head surrounded by curls. I wanted to ask her to take it off so I could see if she looked as good without it but I didn't feel I was in a position where I could make that sort of request. She was a nice woman and the gallery had a good light. She said she'd let me know. And it went on like that until my feet and I were really stinking and I went home to Carmen's where I live and fell into her bath which has claws for feet and damn near wept. Then Carmen came home from school and got in too though I told her I stank and things got better.

That's the trouble I suppose. Nothing else matters, though I'm painting better than I've ever painted because of her. I always wonder about poor buggers like Van Gogh who never sold anything or only one while he lived. How did he keep knowing he was good? I don't see much point in posterity. Did he know he was great or did he just slog on, obsessed with nothing but the next stroke of paint. OK, he had vision, but that doesn't answer the question. I'd really like to know the answer but there is no one to ask. I could ask the man in the suit maybe. He would give some sort of answer probably but we'll never know. Not really.

*

I touch Cliff's bare foot with mine. 'Let's go for a swim,' I say once more.

He looks up, blinking.

'Swim!' I demonstrate, clawing the air with my arms.

He swings his legs up on the sofa. Cliff has good legs, like Edna Everage and my brother Stephen, who says he has the best legs in Hawke's Bay.

Cliff drags up one foot to pick the big toenail. Toenail checked out, he sits up. 'I think I'll go to the store first,' he says.

'What the hell, we've just arrived.'

'Yeah, but that guy, the dealer guy, he said he'd drop me a card, care of the store. I said we were going to be here and he said . . .'

'He won't.'

Cliff looks at me, not pleased. His mouth tightens. 'He said he would.'

'Yes, but people say, people say, people say!' My hands are all over the place trying to disperse my previous negative comment.

'It's not important to him, see,' I explain to my lover who is not in fact handicapped.

'It's only important, the speed, to you.' The sands of non-support move beneath me. I bog deeper in the mire of not understanding a thing about it.

'I'm going.' Cliff leaps to his feet and goes. I read the *Kapiti Observer*. I like the For Sales best. You can pick up anything.

He is back in five minutes flat. He leaps in the French doors and seizes me. He flings cushions. If he could do a backward somersault of delight like the decathlon man he would. He can't contain himself. He is beside himself with joy.

'Let's have a look,' I say, seizing the card. The man in the furry bear suit wishes to mount an exhibition of my lover's work.

I share Cliff's joy and all is harmony and better than that, I shouldn't wonder.

He stops in the middle of a strong clutch and pulls back. 'It'll be a ton of work,' he says. 'This guy's good.' He stares through my head. 'I'll need three nudes,' he mutters. 'Three at least, I'd say.'

His gaze refocuses on my face. He looks at me. 'Oils. Of you.'

I smile, muscles clench. 'Three?' I say.

'At least.'

'Let's go for a swim,' I say yet again.

And we go, leaping down the track, up the track, down the track through the marram grass; sand flying, wind tugging, tumbleweed on the scoot. We are yelling as we fall into the sea which can solve everything. All frustration, all longing, all despair, the sea can cure but only when you're in it. When I am old I will live by the sea and potter about poking at things with a stick and watching the young. When I am dead I will live in it.

We swim naked.

We make love afterwards on Sooze and Bryce's bed. The room smells musty, like the bach bedrooms of childhood when you brushed sand from the soles of your feet with flattened palms before climbing into your bunk.

Nothing wrong with the action though. Cliff is even more charged with creative imagination than usual. I love him dearly.

17

'We could celebrate,' he says afterwards. He picks up my hand and inspects it. 'Celebrate,' he tells it. 'Make a booking at that restaurant in the village.'

I roll over to bite his ear. 'What's it called?'

'I can't remember,' he says.

But we remember later. We make a booking and we go clutching our BYO. The restaurant has a theme and the theme is sport. The wall by the entrance shows cricket memorabilia. An Edwardian child in knickerbockers presents a straight bat. There are framed and autographed photographs of other straight batters and strong bowlers. Several of them have moustaches. There is an old etching of the Hambledon cricket ground.

The other wall is rugby. More moustaches, photographs, deathless tries. I like sport, I'm not knocking it. I like playing it. It is just that here the images are trapped like beetles in kauri gum.

There is a mural in the main room. Pale mauves, lilacs and greens define shadowy figures, most of which are static. Men in white stand near the crease, sit in the pavilion with hats on, converse. Up the rugby end they tackle and fall on their faces. The heads of the figures are transparent, defined by outlines, you can see the dark or light green bushes through them. Cliff is interested in the murals, which he finds effective – as murals. He whips out his sketch pad and begins drawing.

I read the menu. I read that our hosts are called Trevor and Fay and that the restaurant is on the corner of Titoki and West Streets, which we already know.

There is a slice of lemon in the water carafe beside our bottle of Te Mata Estate White, which the waitress has

18

opened. It is not full, the restaurant. One table has a lone male diner with fluffy white hair curling over the back of his collar. He eats slowly, entertaining himself.

Cliff has his pad beneath the table as he sketches a party, if you can call it that, of five. There are two middle-aged men, one handsome, one had it, who sits squeezed and bosomy inside a souvenir shirt labelled *Fiji* with a hibiscus surround. One woman's lilac spectacle frames match the blotched flowers on her frock. She tries to keep up with the men, who are laughing and having fun. The two women opposite have given up. One wears her hair screwed on top in American Gothic style. Flamenco dancers flaunt on her cream jersey silk. She is sick of being here. Gran tells me this happens when you get old. You get sick of it and wonder why you came, though this can happen when you are young and often does.

The rain is hosing down outside, water slams against the windows. The blades of one of the overhead fans on the ceiling move faster than the other. They must be on different settings.

'Well,' I say, lifting my glass to Cliff. 'Here's to the exhibition.'

Cliff has a beautiful smile. It happens comparatively rarely and it pleases me to watch the lips part, the dent in one cheek deepen, the eyes gleam. Rarity has value. People used to get excited when Dylan Thomas turned up sober.

'Yeah,' replies Cliff, lifting his glass to clink mine. He reads the menu. 'Do you want your oysters *en crêpe* or looking at you?'

'Looking at me.'

The door opens. Thundering past the memorabilia, damp with rain and slapping one another, comes a party of

19

eight. They are drunk, these young men. Their faces are red, their clothes are a mess, their feet stumble as they weave around the table laughing and groping for chairs. They are happy. The eyes of the other diners concentrate on their plates except for the lone male diner who has not yet noticed their behaviour. The waitress, smiling strongly, ushers them to a table alongside ours. One of the young men focuses on me. 'Shit,' he informs. 'Get a load of that lot.'

Eight pairs of glazed eyes turn in my direction. Eight drunken hoons gape, their mouths slightly open. They are not a pretty sight.

I order oysters *au naturel* and venison that something time-consuming has happened to. The waitress is very pleasant. I think she must be Fay because she cares so much. She wears the type of long apron worn by French waiters, which is not a good idea because her stomach sticks out and is clamped and bound by the stiff fabric. Periodically she glances at the hoons and gives a quick smile as though she meant them to happen. She takes Cliff's order and moves on to more dangerous territory. She is patient, amiable, she smiles into their stunned-mullet eyes in her attempt to pretend that all is well; that they are civilised welcome guests at mine hosts' (Fay and Trevor's) table. It is uphill work. She moves around explaining; smiling as they order, shout, hit each other, belch, drag bottles of wine from a chilly bin and slam them on the table. They make gestures behind her back to indicate that though she is old enough for kissing she is too fat to tango.

I am getting angry.

'Cliff,' I say.

He is sketching again, his hand moves with authority, he

glances with swift stealthy up and downs of his head at the table of five. Even upside down I can see that he has got the spare dignity and resignation of the American Gothic woman to perfection.

'Nnn?' he says.

'Cliff!'

His hand is still moving. 'Yes?'

I wriggle my shoulders and indicate the table next door with a sideways jerk of the head. 'Drunk,' I hiss.

'Certainly looks like it,' he says, and carries on sketching.

My eyes meet those of the lone male diner. He picks up his lilac napkin and presses it against one corner of his mouth then the other. He returns the napkin to his lap, places his hands on the table and stares at them. He reminds me of something.

I remember. Barry who ditched me and I were staying in a motel in Tauranga where the dining-room invited us to enjoy our smorgasbord in a family atmosphere. The salads were inventive: kumara and bacon, tamarillo and red cabbage, brown rice. There was a lot of kiwifruit. There was kiwifruit in every salad, slices of kiwifruit decorated the plates of cold meat, the pavlovas, the fruit salads and the trifle. It was the ultimate kiwifruit experience. At a table beneath a firehose decorated with a frizzled tinsel wreath left over from Christmas sat two men, one older than the other. The older man's sparse hair was swept across his scalp. He had a tip-tilted nose and a gold chain. He was ashamed of smoking. He took furtive puffs behind one curved hand. He spilt ash and swept it from the table with quick brushing movements of the same hand. The young man's fingers fanned between their faces, dispersing smoke. The older man pressed food. The younger man ate. There was no conversation. The young man had a good haircut, his Docksides were splayed at ten to three. When he was not eating, his hands were clasped together or hung down in despair. He was offered treats, sweets for the sweet. He ate two helpings of trifle decorated with kiwifruit and they departed in silence. It was infinitely sad.

I smile at the silver-haired man. He dips his head but does not smile back. He raises his eyebrows in agreement. He does not enjoy the hoons either.

The noise is increasing at the table next to ours. One man, all red hair and ears, is telling us in song that there's a bridle hanging on the wall, there's the shoes that his old pony wore. If we ask him why those teardrops fall, it's that bridle hanging on the wall. A man with a mean moustache is telling a story with a lot of fucks and ducks in it. All the men are drinking like fishes, except that fishes are breathing when they gulp. Someone throws a roll. There is uproar at the table.

The good-looking man at the table of five summons the waitress, who is looking distracted. She spreads her hands wide in answer to his complaint. Her body language tells me what she is saying. What can she and Trevor do? They didn't know when they took the booking that they would be like this, did they.

His outrage informs her that someone ought to do something and smartly. 'The proprietor,' he mouths. She looks even more miserable but moves quickly to the kitchen, presumably in search of Trevor.

Trevor does not appear.

I am fidgeting about on the seat of my chair in rage and shame for them all. Cliff is totally oblivious. He is now sketching the particular way the silver curls fall on the collar of the jacket of the lone diner, who sits very still staring straight in front of him.

'Good one!' the table roars at the punchline of the fuck and duck story.

'Down trou!' someone screams. The redhead staggers to his feet. Pale and sweating, his head down, he fumbles with his belt. His trousers and underpants fold about his ankles. His hairy white buttocks are presented for inspection two yards from my face. The table roars its approval.

I am on my feet. So is the lone diner.

I haven't been watching. I sense that Carmen is getting a bit toey but the sketch is going so well and I want just a few more minutes and then I'll stop sketching and we'll celebrate and rejoice in each other, which is what we have come for, I do realise that.

I glance up from my pad. The camp man with the silver hair has disappeared from his chair. The table of five is in shock, their knives and forks clutched in mid-air. Carmen has disappeared. There's a lot of noise. I see some guy's bum for a second before he pulls up his trousers amid thundering applause from the rest of them. Carmen and the old gay are standing side by side in front of the table. Carmen is flaming. Someone has lit her fire.

'Get out,' she hisses. 'Now!'

Their obscene comments on her beauty melt on wet lips. They stare. Their mouths are slack. The old man puts one hand on her arm.

'I think perhaps the young lady is upset,' he says gently.

He stacks their half-empty bottles upright in the chilly bin with care. He smiles at them all. 'Why don't you leave now,' he suggests. 'The kitchen will give you corks for the bottles. There's a good takeaway just round the corner on Highway One. And please,' he begs with clasped hands, 'please take taxis home.' He slips a twenty-dollar bill into the chilly bin beside the bottles. He looks at them benignly. 'You are too young to die,' he tells them.

Now they will kill him. There will be a gay bashing. I leap up ten minutes too late.

Not so. The table crawl to their feet and stumble out clutching their liquor. They do not say anything. They do not look at the old man or Carmen. I am still standing, one hand on the chair, the edge of the seat digging into the backs of my knees as they go out the door.

Carmen and the old man turn to each other. They shake hands. He waves one hand towards his table; he asks the jittery waitress for another glass. He holds the chair back for Carmen to sink into. He pours her some wine, showing her the label as he does so. They lean towards each other with their arms on the linen cloth. They talk together, nodding occasionally. They smile.

Living on the Beach

S he stopped the car, climbed out stiffly and opened the gate. It swung wide, clunking against the radiator.

'Nearly there,' she said, backing the car away from the pursuing arc.

'Hh.'

He had an infinity of small sounds to express things he couldn't be bothered saying. Mind the radiator, about time too, or just a noise to indicate continued existence. He clung to the door handle for support as they bucketed up the gravel drive. The ngaios tossed and lurched in the wind, teasing the roof of the car, flinging leaves across the paspalum. The grass that saved the North, a man had told her years ago as they rolled in it. The old man began tugging as she switched off the engine.

'Undo me, Mary.'

'Press the red thing.'

'Where?'

'There.'

'Which?' A vague hand groped by his side, his eyes straight ahead.

She pressed the release and the belt sucked back.

'Oh.'

Her mind flicked to Maud and George, snug and smug in the Hutt. But kind, so kind, to lend the bach, dim faces beaming as they handed over the keys. 'It'll make a change, Mary.'

She climbed out and put the Yale key in the lock. It wouldn't turn. A prickle of panic brushed her as she flung herself against the paint-blistered door.

'Try the other key,' he piped.

Sweating slightly, she did so. The door opened to reveal a concrete block wall, airlessness, and a flight of wooden steps leading above.

'I'll never get up those.'

'It'll be all right, Dad. Just wait while I unpack.'

Some cardboard cartons are better than others. Some are too deep, some, of course, too small. She dumped the sturdy Family Recipe Cake Mix on the sloping bench and stared around her.

The cottage was made of fibrolite flung together on concrete blocks. The main room had budded off four smaller clones, kitchen and bathroom beside the steep stairwell, two bedrooms at the other end. Two elderly armchairs, Maud and George, squatted either side of the doll-sized fireplace which was lined with yellow bricks. Above the mantelpiece hung a faded reproduction of an English wood awash with bluebells, a damp stain creeping down the pale mount. Beneath it a line of shells trekked across the shelf to the glass jar on which laughing peanuts played cricket. The cotton-wool heads of the bunch of harestail it contained were thick with dust. There were two more hardbacked chairs and an unyielding divan covered with a brown rug. An extremely dirty green carpet lay on

26

the floor. The wind flung itself at the front of the house which faced the sea, the draughts making little puffs among the sand drifts on the sills.

But outside was the sea, from every window.

Mary dumped her bag in the pink shoebox bedroom. As she straightened up, she glimpsed her face in a square of mirror which hung from a nail beside the bed. Her hand moved to tuck a strand of hair behind her ear. She remained staring, searching that face.

The other room had two bunks and little else. She sniffed, then opened the window. The mouse lay in a corner, having chosen not to die in the open. Lifting it by the stiff tail, she threw the corpse onto the paspalum to await future burial.

'Mary.' The reedy cry echoed in the stairwell.

'I'm coming.'

First she heaved him out of the car seat, into which he seemed to have collapsed like a punctured beanbag.

'One, two, three, heave!'

'You heaved on three.'

Her laugh turned to a snort. 'I did not.'

I like snorters, the man had told her. Snorters enjoy life, he said.

She held the old man while he stamped some life back into his numbed feet. They were long and slim, their nails fortunately not horny. They began the climb. She supported him from behind, pausing at each step as he fought for breath. 'Phrrr, Phrrr, Phrrr.' What little breath he had all seemed to puff outwards.

'I'll never make it.'

'Don't talk.'

They reached the top and he collapsed on one of the hard chairs, mottled blue face in his hands.

'Whisky.'

It was at the ready in the hutch-like kitchen. She slopped some into a glass, added a splash of water and placed it in the groping hand.

'Mad. Mad. Shouldn't have come.'

'You're here now. Don't worry.'

'Never get up there again. Never.'

'You won't have to. Look, there's the island. And the sea.'

They turned to watch their common interest, rolling and sucking at the sand below. The rough weather had tossed the sea into vast stripes of green, steel blue, and . . . ultramarine. Of course.

She had never seen him in the water. Childhood memories of learn-to-swim campaigns had never included his arms. He had loved to be in boats tossing in water which made her sick. They stared at the repetitive unforgiving sea.

'I can't see it,' he said.

She turned to him. He had recovered what little breath he had and sat sipping his whisky with dignity, long legs crossed above the knee, the upper hanging parallel. Not many men sat as well, she had noticed. Their crossed legs were a collection of protruding bits, no symmetry in the assemblage. His hands, like his feet, remained satisfactory. When he moved them, the long fingers often made an acute angle with the bony wrists. Flexibility remained there, and beauty. She remembered her mother . . .

'He could have done anything with those hands.'

An insane thing to say, and he hadn't.

28

Mary moved about the cottage with precision, scrubbing the smell of mouse to extinction, making beds and stowing gear.

'You'll be better in here, Dad. The bunk's nice and low.'

'Where's the lavatory?'

Her arm swept in the direction. 'Here.'

'Where?'

She flapped her outstretched hand. 'Here,' she said.

'Miles away.'

Their days settled into a rhythm. Meals followed meals in an orderly procession, little nap followed little nap, much as at home. He appropriated the divan and its rug and lay staring out the window, searching for the sea. Or slept, a crumpled heap of brown. Occasionally he jerked, or gave a stifled yelp like an old dog asleep by a fire.

Mary lived on the beach. She could hear her future grateful voice as she returned the keys to Maud. 'I lived on the beach. It was wonderful.'

There were not many occupied baches, no store, all the children were back at school. She swam twice a day, her square figure encased in a bathing suit aglow with hot flowers, her head in an orange rubber cap. Every day she braced herself against the damp shock of stretch nylon, then ploughed through the sculpted sandhills to the waves. She floated over unbroken ones, or swam at them, head on, to surge over the top, defeating the crashing roar behind her.

After he was settled, a word often in her mind, she turned right and walked for miles along the beach, conscientiously adding to the driftwood pile by the back door on her return.

About a quarter of a mile along the beach to the right, a

bach stood alone. Marram grass had been planted in the drifting sand in front, taupata and ngaios ringed the section – like the green scribbled hedge of a child's drawing. On the beach below the house, a man and his golden retriever played each morning. Except that you couldn't call it playing.

'Heel!' roared the man.

The dog responded by hurling towards him, flinging itself slobbering against the godhead, its tail a plume of gold.

'Sit!'

It dropped on its haunches, eyes beseeching the next clue, ears pricked, tail lifting.

It was usually 'Stay!', after which the man walked away from the quivering mass crouched on the damp sand. But at the slightest lift the man would turn. 'I said Stay!'

'He seems to enjoy it,' she said one day.

'It's obedience training.' The wind was blowing strands of faded red hair across his face.

'Oh. What's his name?'

'Rusty.'

She rubbed the dog behind the right ear. It opened its jaws wide, yawing at her wrist, trying to catch the agent of ecstasy. Its wet frilled black gums reminded her of the dark insides of a paua shell.

'He's very obedient.'

'Him! Lord no, he's only a pup. It takes months. Or years.'

She smiled a beach meeter's token smile and walked on.

The next time she stopped to watch, the man had a rolled-up newspaper in his hand.

'Down!' he yelled, hitting the dog's nose with the teaching aid. Then he called, 'Come on, you fool.'

Each day their walks became longer. The glistening hardness stretched before them as the dog gambolled, the only word. It chased gulls, which obligingly arced into the air. The oystercatchers could hardly be bothered, but at the last gasp they lifted from their fussy comic run into long straight flight along the tide line, screaming to each other, Kee-eep, Kee-eep.

He talked easily. His wife had been a true blonde, never touched it, women always asked her what she used, they couldn't believe it was natural. It was though. After she'd died he'd felt completely lost. Completely. Mary told him little. There was little to tell and she was a reticent woman. She had taught English for many years, and now she looked after her father. Yes.

Companionable silences followed amiable comments. They agreed that a walk without a dog is not the same, that it seemed a pity that the best weather always came after the children had gone back to school. He told her about the time he'd been sent to the UK on a course, he'd been lucky to get it, and how he could hardly stand it, being so bloody lonely. There used to be a cigarette advertisement: 'You're never alone with a Something.' He couldn't even remember the name.

'Next day,' he said, eyes disappearing as he grinned, 'I went out and bought a packet of Somethings.'

The dog was investigating a dead fish, sniffing and barking at the mouldering carcase above the tide line.

'Heel!' Rusty lifted his head and careered towards them.

'Good dog.' His hand slid over the shining, sycophantic head.

31

'Now I feel like that about the sea,' he said.

She stopped, staring at him, the tide licking at her jandals.

'I must get back to Dad,' she murmured.

She tried to remember when the sun had shone so continuously. She had to go back to her childhood, to days of dried paddling rings around the scaly brown legs of endless summers. The weather broke but the walks continued, parkas dripping, rain spitting the sand.

He asked about her father.

'He's very old,' she said.

'Can I come and say Hullo to the old boy?'

She cut the walk short and stumped home, brushing the rain from her eyes.

'His name's Don McIndoe, Dad,' she said next day, checking his jersey for major spills.

'Hhh.'

But the old man was sitting on the straight-backed chair, waiting, when Don crashed through the front door in a scud of rain. It was the first time she had seen him without Rusty.

Talk immediately ballooned between the two men, fishing talk, shared memories of the Tongariro, the lakes, other rivers. Her father bummed a cigarette, triumphantly not coughing. He told Don that one of the pleasures of old age, almost the only one, Hh Hh, was remembering, in exact detail mind, almost every cast he'd made when catching a fresh-run hen, fifty, no sixty years ago, in the Major Jones Pool. It happened quite often, those sudden sharp complete memories. Don said he'd look forward to that. The old man grinned, his mouth a weathered slit. He gripped the edge of his chair, lifted his behind fractionally and jerked nearer his friend, his eyes leaking with joy. They turned to rugby, controversial decisions, hard, bruising games, brushing aside proffered nuts as though they were uninvited flies.

The rain had stopped. A stream of dense grey clouds poured across the sky to the south. The low ones disappeared behind the island as though pulled behind a black cardboard cut-out. Time passed. She rose to fill the glasses again.

'I'll get Don a drink,' he said. Levering himself up, gasping slightly, he stamped his feet into action.

She sat down on Maud. The noise was only a dropped glass but the spell was broken. The old man shuffled back and collapsed on the divan, tugging at the fringe of the rug.

A sensible man, Don suggested leaving by the back door to avoid sand blasting them again with the northerly. She followed him silently downstairs and shook hands like a hostess. His skin was tough and dry, his eyes bright.

'Great old guy. If I can be like that at his age . . . See you in the morning, Mary. Thanks a lot.'

He ran off down the drive. She wondered for a moment if he would jump the gate, then remembered it was open.

She climbed the stairs slowly, pulling on the wooden banister.

She woke next morning and lay watching the sunspot reflection from the mirror jigging on the ceiling. One two, up and back, one two . . . She heard her father creeping to the lavatory, the clunking pull of the chain, the rushing sound of the water followed by the dragging whisper of his slippers' return. She pulled a jersey and trousers over her pyjamas and crept downstairs, opened the back door and floundered through the sandhills to the sea.

At the water's edge she turned left towards the river. Her hair streamed back from her face in permed rats'-tails as she quickened her pace. 'Frankie and Johnnie were lovers,' she bellowed. 'Oh Lordy how they could love,' she roared at the wind which snagged each word upwards, outwards, away, in snatches of diminishing sound as she strode along the beach.

The Right Sort of Ears

Why, thought the poet sourly, am I here? I should go home. 'Return to my mountains of light and mauve melancholy.' Just piss off.

He looked around him, glancing left, right, and left again beneath lowered eyelids. The effect was to make his face inscrutable, or rather more so. The expression on his well-planned face had been non-commital since early youth. The darting glances, the heavy lids, merely increased its air of detachment, almost, one could say, its reptilian aspect. One would not have been surprised, or not as surprised as usual, to have seen a forked tongue flick lightning-fast then disappear. Such astonishments are seldom seen, but poets are different from others and this one was more different than most.

And why had the wretched people chosen this place for interrogation? Outdoors; shadowed by trees and deep in sparrows, crumbs, and clutter, the place left much to be desired. Pigeons, pigeons for God's sake, were swooping. The place was alive with hazards. A downtown café they had called it. A downtown café with knobs on.

He looked at the blackboard menu on the wall and found no comfort. Focaccia with hummus, beetroot, tofu and pan-roasted vegetables, smoked chicken and avocado salad, bacon, tomato and lettuce salad, cream cheese, kiwi fruit and God knows what salad. As always, there were repellent muffins; broccoli and feta cheese, cauliflower, brie and sesame seeds. And buns. Buns to the right of them, buns to the left of them. Bagels were present.

How had it come about, this dreadful food? he wondered. Why had he not noticed this infuriating lurch towards health and indigestible muck before it was too late? Where was the food of his youth; the chop and the sausage; the pie, the pea and the pud? The glories of the Pie Cart, the chips with everything had suited him well, and now look at it.

Recently he had attended a dinner after some Writers and Readers shindig and found, to his pleasure but not surprise, that he was seated next to the guest of honour. Miss Phoebe Glass was a poet of international renown, a woman of intellectual vigour and at ease with words. He had hoped for intelligent converse with this handsome being, an exchange of sentiments, a marriage of true minds to which no one would have the nerve to admit impediment. This had not happened. Miss Glass had talked about little else other than her indigestion. She did enquire, not tenderly, no one could call it tenderly, but at least she had asked whether he suffered from this complaint. When he said no, she had sighed, had left him sitting beside her belch-free and heartburn-negative, had picked up the conversational reins and cantered on. The pain, she said, the sleepness nights. She discussed alternative palliatives available and their comparative efficacy, she gave him names – Slowburn, Quickees, and all shades between. She couldn't, she told him, move without them. She rummaged in her bag, produced a packet of tablets and sucked a couple before resuming her wistful poking at a side salad.

The poet smiled his reptilian smile. 'Bismuth before pleasure,' he murmured.

Miss Glass gave him a long cool stare and turned a shoulder.

They were late, these people. Americans are meant to be punctual, to appreciate, to astound you with the depth of their perceptions, their sensitivity to the more arcane aspects of your work. But above all to be punctual. Where the hell were they?

He gave more glances to right and left. Not a glimpse of them: no one beneath the artificial palm, nobody crouching behind the nude female statue who drooped beside a small and dingy pool.

The nude was made of concrete; the grey lumps of her breasts seemed to have been slapped on to the rest of her arbitrarily, without any reference or knowledge, let alone admiration for the female form. He could imagine the scene. A handful of concrete this side, Bong! And another over here to match, Bong! Now she's apples.

The result depressed him. These rounded orbs of beauty, these concrete hills of passion with protuberant mud-grey nipples, were as extraneous, as sexless and oddly attached to the torso as those of Michelangelo's figures of Night and Dawn in his Tombs of the Medici in Florence. He remembered standing before them many years ago, discussing the topic with his then wife, Mildred.

'Very odd. Do you think it was because he was a homosexual?'

'No,' said Mildred. 'I think it was because he couldn't do breasts.'

Nor could this one. Useless.

There were, understandably, not many other people in the place. Even waitresses were few and far between. One with an exuberant mass of yellow hair had asked if she could take his order. He had explained the position and she had departed, virtually skipping with the relief of it all.

In one corner sat two women, sisters without a doubt. Grey-haired, pleasant, and faded to monotones, they were sharing a large slice of carrot cake. One wore wheat on sand, the other pink on rose. They put sugar in their respective cappuccinos and giggled. The poet knew, as surely as though they had semaphored the intelligence to him with small coloured flags, that they did not normally take sugar, that this was a treat and why not. Life, they signalled, was for living.

At a table nearer to hand sat Father, Mother, and two small girls. Again the occupants of this table were neatly dressed and somewhat anachronistic in appearance. Both Father and Mother were bluff, portly, dark-suited and well shod. The twins, for such they must be, wore dresses which could have been designed for the little princesses Lilibet and Margaret Rose. They were blue, these frocks, they were smocked, they had bows. They were as identical as their blond-haired wearers who sat eating cake and being good. Their fork work was competent and their white socks had frills.

Nevertheless, they palled. The poet glanced at his watch. Bugger this. He had half risen to his feet when he was engulfed, overwhelmed by a tsunami of apologies which began at the door, surged forward and knocked him sideways. Harold and Bea Benderman couldn't begin to say how sorry they were. They had gotten lost, would you believe. Could the poet ever forgive them? They had walked to the Art Gallery and gotten lost. Their arms indicated astonishment, their knees, their whole bodies, begged for pardon.

'Not at all,' said the poet. 'Shall we sit down?'

They sat, they ordered, they smiled. Harold explained to the waitress that he wanted hot chocolate with water not milk. The young woman was puzzled. Even her hair looked startled. 'Like no milk at all?'

'Like no milk at all.'

'Not even cold?'

'Nope. Just a bagel.'

'Not even the marshmallow?'

'Pardon me?'

'You get a free marshmallow.'

Harold raised a hand. 'Hold it.'

She gave up. 'OK,' she said and drifted away.

'We can only hope,' murmured the poet, now grooming himself in preparation for questions. A hand wiped each side of his head, one carried on to smooth his front hair forward.

The odd thing was, he thought, his eyes still flicking and his mouth firm, that Harold and his sister, Bea Benderman, were so alike. The place seemed to be filling up with clones, twinned identi-kits, double-goers. Harold and Bea (first names, please) both had flat faces. They had flat little noses, flat foreheads and almost non-existent chins. Their ears were flat, their hair was fair and their eyes were small. The poet was reminded of photographs demonstrating the

39

flat profiles of maggots; the straight fronts of railcars; the sliced-off ends of sidewalk canopies.

'Of course, Doctor,' said Harold, after some discussion had taken place, 'I'm thinking that your place in posterity is assured. There can be no doubt about that. And I'm wondering whether you would you care to tell me how you feel about this?'

Oh God. The poet gave a small crank-up cough. 'I have nothing against posterity,' he said.

Harold and Bea laughed merrily. Harold stopped first. 'Your body of work, its universal excellence, the respect in which your entire oeuvre is held throughout the world, both in academia, and,' a hand tossed, 'the general public. You even,' confided Harold, '*sell*.'

The poet stared at his boots. 'Yes,' he said.

Harold leaned forward. He wore a gold chain around his neck. Why would a man with a flat face wear such a thing?

'Can I ask a question?' asked Bea, her small eyes bright with daring.

'Please do.'

'Why is it, do you think, that your poetry is so universally admired?'

The poet glanced at the concrete maiden. The sands were running, the tide would soon be on the turn, there could well be whitebait. 'Summertime, and the livin' is easy.' Or should be.

He made a major effort, looked into her eyes and smiled. Her face, when he looked at it closely, was not as flat as her brother's. It was longer, finer, a serene medieval face with unexpectedly bright eyes. He looked with attention at her ears. As he had hoped, they not only lay

40

flat against her head, but were lobeless. He had always had a weakness for lobeless medieval ears. He could not lie to those ears.

'Because,' he said, 'it's good.'

Bea clapped her hands, gave a little bounce. 'Sure,' she said. 'But *why* is it so good?'

'Because I can do words. I can find the right ones to say what I need.'

Her long neck drooped, a hand touched her mouth. 'Could you enlarge on that a little, Doctor? Harold and I have both always been so . . . well, it's just so mind-blowing to even like, meet you, let alone *talk*.'

There must be something sensible he could say. 'I do a lot of thinking,' he said finally. 'Is that any help?'

'To find *le mot juste*?' yelped Harold.

'Yes. And *la pensée*.'

It was now Harold who was bouncing about. '"What oft was thought, but ne'er so well expressed"?' he cried.

'If you say so,' said the poet. He smoothed his front hair once more. 'Nice word "ne'er", I must look it up.'

'It'll just say "poet or arch,"' murmured Bea.

She seemed to have gone rather wistful. He must help her. 'Tell me some words you like, Bea.'

'Sundance, quicksilver, heartsease.'

'For Chrissake, Bea,' snapped Harold, 'don't go all peasbody on us.'

The poet did not enjoy seeing a woman discomfited, especially a serious, gentle woman with the right sort of ears. He smiled at her. 'There's nothing wrong with the word "peasbody" as long as it is taken to mean the body of a pea. I can't say I care for it as a name.'

Bea smiled back. Between them, unexpected and

munificent as light from glow-worms, flowed sympathy, understanding, empathy – all the good ones. Harold was on the outer, a dead duck in need of plucking.

'Tell me some words you don't like,' said Bea.

They were interrupted by a minor commotion from beside the pool. The two small girls were inspecting the naked lady. One of them put out a tentative hand to stroke a concrete breast. The other, overcome with giggles, snatched it away. 'Mummy,' she squealed, 'Ella's going to touch the lady's boosies, and she shouldn't, should she, Mummy?'

Ella gave the sneak a passing swipe and danced back to the table.

'Rosie,' called Mother. 'Come here.'

Rosie went.

The poet put one hand over Bea's long, tapering fingers. 'Boosies,' he said, 'is a disaster. Promise me, Beatrice, you will never use the word "boosies".'

'I promise.' Beatrice glanced at their hands for a second and laughed. Her voice lightened, her bright eyes snapped. 'Tell me more words,' she said. 'All the words you know. Tell me.'

I Thought There'd Be a Couch

D r Celia Crowe is switched on and well presented.
A super-slim Rolex hides her left wrist, a small-
linked gold bracelet lies alongside, an antique
watch-chain circles her neck, the toggle lying in the dip at
the base of her throat. Her skirt is not visible below her
desk but her legs are. Close together, slanted side by side
like the Queen's, they lie pale and interesting in 15-denier.
Her feet are small, hidden inside black patent-leather shoes
with miniheels and flat grosgrain bows. They are so shiny
you could see her pants in them, but this Standard Four
vernacular is forgotten. The caramel linen jacket she wears
is pleated and padded on the shoulders like that of a
Samurai warrior. It fastens with brass buttons. When Dr
Crowe stands it hangs well below her hips and she looks
fashionably top heavy. She wears her hair pinned up
during consultations. When she loosens it, leaping black
curls spring from their confinement. There is so much to
stow away that the effect, when she is working, is of
exuberance controlled but not repressed.

Dr Crowe used to be an active feminist but after fifteen
years of slaving night and day to attain her position as a
psychiatrist in private practice, sisterhood has gone down

43

the tubes. Dr Crowe is an Uncle Tom; one of the boys, professionally speaking.

Mr Huxtable has never been one of the boys. He sits very still in one of the uncomfortable chairs in Dr Crowe's waiting-room. They are so overstuffed, so unyielding, that he feels like a pea on a drumhead.

The colour scheme is grey and darker grey plus silver with touches of flamingo pink. The knobbly carpet is the weary grey of old porridge, the walls are silver grey, the chairs are dark grey, the scatter cushions are flamingos ranging from palest blush to dark salmon. (Well-fed flamingos, whose diet includes shrimp-like shellfish, are a deeper pink than the disadvantaged.)

The pictures on the walls are reassuring and calm. The one directly in front of Mr Huxtable has splashes of pink flung against what looks to him like wet sand at Waikanae when the tide is out. There is the same sheen, the same silver streaks at the tide line, a black outline which may or may not be Kapiti. Mr Huxtable shuts one eye in his attempt to make a decision. He thinks on balance it must be.

The other picture hangs beside the reception area. A sign saying RECEPTION stands on the bench beside a cardboard cut-out of a red rose on a long stalk, the base of which tells him this is a smoke-free zone. Mr Huxtable turns his attention to the picture. Here silver nymphs dance, silhouetted on the skyline against a huge full moon. A weeping silver birch stands to one side of the last leaping nymph. There is a satyr or two; the procession is led by a round-bellied infant playing upon a medieval musical instrument, the name of which escapes Mr Huxtable, though he did know it once. Trump? Timbal? Not that. He will have to look it up. How though? How will he start when he knows only the shape, which is that of an elongated horn.

Mr Huxtable has been waiting a long time. He looks at the young man opposite him, who is reading what must be a piece of in-depth journalism as he has not lifted his head for forty minutes.

'They think you've got all day,' says Mr Huxtable gently. The young man lifts his head in fright, nods and dives back into his article. His jersey is sage green, his chubby face is pale, his hands fumble as he turns a page.

Mr Huxtable picks up the morning paper. The front page has a photograph of a proud young policeman after his graduation ceremony. He holds a sleeping baby bundled in his arms. The previous week he supported his wife throughout her long and difficult labour. It was thirty hours, he says. He wouldn't have had it any other way, he says. Mr Huxtable sighs. He knows the cop means he is glad to have supported his wife, not pleased her labour was difficult. Don't they hear what they say? Another photograph depicts a doctor on an offshore island which has inadequate consulting-room facilities. One of these days, warns the Doctor, we're going to lose someone we needn't have. Mr Huxtable sighs again, puts down the paper and rubs his knuckles in his eyes. He picks up an Australian magazine which shows red-capped lifesavers marching, places it on the table, lifts his feet onto it and closes his eyes.

'Dr Crowe will see you now, Mr Eddy,' cries the nurse from behind the glass which defines her territory.

The young man ditches the magazine, scrambles to his

feet and lopes to the door indicated by Nurse Mollet. He wears boots which Mr Huxtable's re-opened eyes do not recognise as either farm or army. They are tidy boots of quality, but not fashion. They are workmanlike, the laces twist from knob to knob up his ankles, the toes are blunt and bulbous. They nail Mr Eddy's fantasies to the ground.

'Good luck,' calls Mr Huxtable.

Mr Eddy, appalled, backs through the door. Mr Huxtable shuts his eyes again. Nurse Mollet stares at his feet but says nothing.

Mr Huxtable opens his eyes slowly as Nurse Mollet shakes his shoulder.

'You were asleep.'

His eyes are clear, blue, rimmed with pink lids. 'I'm not now.'

His bald head is freckled and sun-pocked, his curls have retreated to a ring of grey fluff above his ears. Hair sprouts from his nostrils, his ears, from beneath the worn cuffs of his grey cotton shirt.

'Dr Crowe is a very busy person,' says Nurse Mollet. 'Especially taking over Dr Grigg's list like today.'

Mr Huxtable agrees. His voice is soft as he confirms her statement. 'Well, you can see that, can't you,' he says, 'otherwise we wouldn't be sitting round here all day.' He nods at Nurse Mollet's pink-and-grey head and heaves himself out of the chair. The seat of his woollen work trousers hangs in folds about his shrunken old-man's buttocks as he moves to the door. Nurse Mollet recalls the same grey slackness at the zoo as Kamala lurched away, one manacled foot clanking behind another. Her grandson Errol's wave from the swaying howdah was nervous.

Kamala is dead now. Opportunists wanted the ivory but Mr Gartrell the vet insisted the tusks remain intact, buried with the rest of the corpse.

Celia took her car in first thing for an oil change. Margie followed to provide a lift home.

Celia's instructions to the mechanic are quite explicit.

'And make sure you put one of those things on the steering wheel,' she says.

'What things?' asks the blank moustached face.

Why do they always wear white? Like the blood-smeared overalls of late-night meat deliverers. Mad.

'Those things to keep the mess off the wheel,' says Celia, nodding at his blackened hands which tighten around the cheesecloth.

'OK.'

'Last time it was all over me.' Celia flings quick hands at her hair, her chest, towards him, palms wide in demonstration.

'I said, OK.'

Celia gives him a winning smile. 'Five-thirty,' she says. She turns on her heel and marches out of the cavernous clanging dump, past the oil-slicked puddles to Margie's Mini.

They have been friends since Grammar and started Medical School together. Margie and Rob dragged her from beneath the dissecting table when she fainted. The cadavers were memento mori carved from mahogany, the formalin stench all-pervading. It got into your clothes, hair, fingers. Cameras were forbidden but later Rob took a snap of her dissecting out Bert's laryngeal nerve. Rob was also on Bert. Some of the men were full of innuendos and

47

sexual cracks during dissection. Not Rob. He appeared in third-year after a year off to sort himself out. He spoke only when he had something to say. People found it disconcerting. He's hard to know, they said.

The three of them went to pubs together, handed on news of the best takeaways, op shops, likely exam questions and model answers. Rob had an old Escort and Margie sat in the front passenger's seat. One day she found herself in the back and Rob and Celia have lived together ever since. Six months ago they bought a house in Mount Victoria and one day Rob will unpack completely. Celia realises he is swotting but God in Heaven, can't he see she can't live like this? Not when it's their own house. Rob is at Public and is about to sit his surgery finals for the third time.

Margie leans across to unlock the passenger's door. The parting between the red-gold curls is bright pink. Celia's mother disliked red hair. Her redheaded sister, Celia's Aunty Bet, fell in the sheep dip when she was eight and Celia's mother laughed and laughed.

Margie is in general practice. Her surgery is near Celia and Rob's house and she has agreed to take Celia back to pick up the Honda. Celia has taken the day off to work on a paper entitled 'Sanctuary: An Outdated Concept?' which she is reading at a forthcoming psychiatrists' conference in Queenstown and is worried about.

Celia opens the yellow door of Margie's Mini and ducks in. Her legs swing in in a united sweep. 'Surly brute,' she says.

'Oh well,' says Margie. She leads the gear lever by the hand, her fingers resting on top of the round knob through first and second, beneath to slip into third, on top again to sweep down into fourth. Margie is a good driver. She and Celia have a game called What I am good at. Celia is good at having legible writing and a sense of direction. Margie is good at driving. And she answers letters. Not everyone can play this game. I'm not good at anything, they say, thereby missing the point. One of the talents Celia and Margie share, for example, is for scrubbing floors. They both use plenty of good hot soapy water, get right into the corners and take a pride in doing so. Such shared minor talents increase their empathy and make them laugh.

Margie stops for a red light, her head high. Women, especially women with good profiles, look better driving a car. The world is their oyster. Women don't look so good driving a car with children, as their eyes have to glance about, even with seatbelts, and the alert questing look is dissipated.

'I've thought of another game,' says Margie.

Celia has discovered a hangnail on her thumb. 'Oh, what?'

'What's the main thing you knew during the first seven years of your life? Your main feeling about it.'

Celia gives up trying to snip it off with her front teeth. 'You mean the Jesuit bit? First seven years stuff?'

'Not necessarily Jesuit.'

'Why seven then?'

'All right.' Margie's right foot is down, she is leaping away. 'Make it six if you're fussed.'

'Six. OK.' Celia knows immediately, but two can play at this game. 'What's yours?'

'I'm working on it,' says Margie. 'Tell me yours.'

'I knew they loved me,' says Celia. 'That I was special.'

49

Margie changes down and swings into Majoribanks
Street which can be either Marsh or Marjorie.

Celia has been working in the spare room for a quarter of
an hour. The floor is bare. Rob's stuff is piled beneath the
double-hung window; clothes are bundled into cartons, old
textbooks lie about. *Medical Jurisprudence* is open at putrefac-
tion, a New World plastic bag contains mixed shoes, two
sleeping bags are dumped beside his squash racquet, which
has two small white feathers caught in its stringing. An
Agee jar contains a Citizen diver's watch without a strap, a
ten-trip bus ticket, a blue ballpoint, an old comb, a red
pencil-sharpener shaped like a die, assorted keys and a
twenty-first wallet. Rob works in the living-room in a cane
chair with a piece of board across his knees and his books
in a wide circle around him. He can only work like that.
Celia's table is an old flush door on trestles, both of which
she bought at a Rotary auction. She gave the door several
coats of gloss polyurethane and its dark shining surface
pleases her. She is working on her statistics, getting them in
order to put them through the practice's computer. The
figures look weird. She picks up her pocket calculator as
the telephone in the hall gives its muted ring.

'Celia Crowe,' she says, squatting down to its level.

'Celia? It's Jenny Mollet.'

'Yes, Jenny.'

'Dr Grigg has flu. He says can you do his surgery list?'

'Oh, *Jenny*.' Celia rolls onto her behind, cradling the
receiver against her face as though she loved the bloody
thing.

'Well yes, I *know*,' the voice wheedles. 'But he's got a full
list and there are some urgent repeats.'

50

Dr Grigg is the psychiatrist with whom Celia shares consulting-rooms. He is an elder statesman, a bosomy cuddle-bunny of a man well loved by his patients.

The soundproofing at the rooms is not perfect. Each day Celia hears Dr Grigg's soothing murmur through the wall, though she doesn't hear the words as he questions, diagnoses, explains and cares for his patients. Celia finds the sound distracting but the architect says the proofing is as specified, no one queried it and Insulfluff wouldn't help. Celia thinks Dr Grigg is dependent on his patients' dependence, but he and Celia respect each other and have an arrangement whereby each will mind the shop for the other in a crisis. Not long-term treatment; just urgent repeats, a hand on the pulse, a keeping of despair at arm's length, or bay if possible. New patients can be a problem. Are they to be returned? This is open for negotiation, but defections are usually accepted with good grace by the absent member of the team.

Celia glances at the large sheaf of papers in her hand. Shit. 'OK, Jenny I'll have to get a taxi, my car's in dock.'

She throws the papers down on her work table. They are abandoned, adrift on a bronze sea. She returns to the hall and punches the taxi numbers with a stiff middle finger. She'll ring Margie from the rooms to change the pick-up arrangements.

The taxi arrives promptly and Celia scrambles to change from jeans to skirt and snatch her briefcase, bag and jacket. She usually has plenty of time and emerges trim as a marching girl in garments assembled from the floor. Rob can never understand why this is different from his mess and Celia thinks his lack of perception is endearing.

The taxi smells of nicotine and a synthetic rose which

seeps from a deodoriser attached to the dashboard. The thing is nearly defunct. Only a half moon of pink deliquescing substance is visible between the slots of white plastic. Celia opens the window.

Last night Margie arrived at Celia and Rob's house with greasies, having got fed up. They ate them sitting on the new wall-to-wall carpet in front of the TV, their backs lined against the pastel weave of the six-foot sofa. Three people on a sofa is more of a straight line than three people on the floor in front of it. People on sofas are framed by sofa, cut off.

There is not much in the room apart from the carpet and the sofa and the cane chair, which has padded cushions aglow with hibiscus and is large and designed for relaxation on patios. Rob's board leans against it and his current textbooks lie open or shut around it. There is a bay window and a mantelpiece of three curved pieces of wood like the Pink and White Terraces before eruption. Rob thinks it's Art Deco. Celia isn't sure but will find out. The curtains which loop and fall are unbleached calico in profusion. There is a leather pouf which Celia's mother was glad to get rid of, stereo equipment, speakers, records and CDs piled high. On the mantelpiece buds of Japanese iris, long and tight and enclosed, reveal slashes of deepest blue at their tips. The heavy glass vase which holds them was Margie's last birthday present to Celia.

Margie has just told them something they hadn't heard about the National Women's Hospital Inquiry, but nothing would surprise them now.

The TV sits on the carpet, blinking through lack of aerial. Periodically, the two doomed whales in Alaska which have captured the attention of the viewing world surface on the screen. A snout appears, breaking the surface of the water. The mouth gapes, the whale gives an ineffective blow, then, infinitely poignant, the blunted snout sinks once more. Inuits and cameramen stand silent about the hole, another snout rises, lifts, then slowly disappears. President Reagan appears on the screen, his eyes sad as he promises that America will do all it can.

'No one would give a stuff if it was three Eskimos,' says Margie, her hand on the Cerebos.

'Two,' corrects Celia.

Margie's eyes shut briefly. 'More salt?' she says to Rob.

Rob shakes his head. 'What did you expect?'

'You're not having more salt?' says Celia.

'A lady doctor like you,' says Rob.

Dimples are evanescent. They appear from nowhere like mushrooms, sometimes before the smile. Margie sprinkles salt, replaces the Cerebos and leans back, still smiling.

'These chips are good,' she says.

'Where're they from?' asks Rob.

'The usual.'

'I thought they'd changed hands,' mutters Rob.

Margie shakes her head, her mouth full.

'Did you see *Nanook of the North*?' asks Celia.

Heads shake. Hands select, abandon, stow.

'They really did ditch them, you know. Old people. They did in the film.'

'When they had no teeth, wasn't it?' says Margie.

'Whatever,' says Celia, rolling fluff from the new carpet into a ball with her fingers.

'Because they couldn't chew, I mean,' says Margie.

'Somewhere in Kurdistan the nomads just leave them

on the other side of the river,' says Rob, scrubbing his face with a paper napkin. 'When you can't make it across you just stay on the wrong side.'

'Of course you'd be conditioned to it,' says Celia. 'I mean, as a child you'd see Granny left, then Grandad. I mean ... Well, you'd know.'

'Yeah,' says Rob. He glances from one face to another. 'Any more?' Margie and Celia shake their heads. Rob screws up the remaining chips inside the paper and stands. From their angle his head seems to touch the light. 'But I reckon however conditioned you are it would be different when it's you.'

'Well of course,' says Celia. 'But you'd still accept it.'

'I wouldn't.'

'Nor me,' says Margie.

'Remember when I had that tendon?' says Rob.

'Yes.'

'I felt like saying to the guy, "This is not some hack you're dealing with. This is me."' He pauses. 'Bugger it, I wouldn't accept anything.'

'You'd have to,' says Celia.

'Yeah, you'd have to but you wouldn't,' says Rob. 'Not when it was you.'

'They put them on icebergs, didn't they?' says Margie.

'Floes,' says Celia.

'Go with the floe.' Rob turns at the door. 'Nescaf OK?'

Margie crosses her legs beneath her and is on her feet tugging at her skirt. 'I'll bring the plates. Hang on.' Rob waits at the door.

Celia comes to with a slight jump. The taxi man is talking. He is Greek. Every morning, he tells Celia, he has

54

instructed his grandson to come to him and say, 'Grandad, remember Roger Douglas.' This is so the driver will not forget his morning hate against the Minister of Finance who ruined the country. A fifth-century BC Persian king, says the driver, slowing for the lights, ordered one of his officers to recite to him each morning, 'Remember the Greeks.'

'But you're teaching your grandson to hate,' says Celia.

The large handsome head nods, the eyes in the mirror are calm, dark as Kalamáta olives. 'That's right,' says the driver.

Celia has prescribed a repeat of lithium for Miss Cullen's chronic depression and a repeat of Serenace for Mr Jiles's psychosis. She has reassured Mrs Goodman that constipation is one of the normal side effects of Sineqan but this can be dealt with, and she will give Mrs Goodman a note for the chemist with the name of the laxative that she is sure Dr Grigg would recommend, though, as Mrs Goodman is probably aware, laxatives are no longer on the prescription list. Yes, it is unfair. She thinks probably the reason Dr Grigg didn't warn Mrs Goodman is that it's not always a side effect. She has suggested to Mr Eddy that he should ask Dr Grigg about group-counselling therapy, which she has found helpful for patients of hers with similar problems. Mr Eddy's white face tightens. He says he'll think about it and leaves quickly. Celia makes another note.

A young woman in a denim miniskirt hops on one leg with glee as she leaves the Medical Centre next door. Pregnancy test negative? Or positive perhaps? A child in a padded yellow anorak and minuscule jeans pads past attached to an old woman with pink-tinted hair. The child points. The pink head nods.

Celia turns back to Mr Eddy's mental history. Her writing is blue-black italic, modified for speed. She spent hours at Grammar sitting in the back row perfecting the narrow upstrokes and wide downward sweeps which give style to her hand. The rest of Five A thought she was mad. Her pen came from Henlow and Jenkins of Jermyn Street. J. Fyfe pp James Spence despatched her black Mont Blanc. He enclosed a typewritten note suggesting she stick to Quink. The pen's shape is that of a small fat torpedo and cost the earth.

The door opens and Mr Huxtable enters. Celia sees a small unknown man and registers the secret 'new patient' snip of pleasure. She smiles at Mr Huxtable and stows Mr Eddy's notes away.

'Mr Huxtable,' she says. 'Do sit down.'

Mr Huxtable remains standing in front of her. He stares gravely around her pleasant consulting-room, which is Edwardian in concept. There is a large wooden cabinet which houses exotic shells collected in Samoa by Celia's Uncle Ted. An antique grandfather chair upholstered in dark green Dralon awaits the patient. A round footstool embroidered in white, grey and black beads sits beside it. The carpet is grey. The desk is new. There are no pictures.

'I thought there'd be a couch,' says Mr Huxtable.

Celia's bottom teeth are visible as her smile widens. 'Did you?' she says.

'You haven't got a proper desk either.'

Celia's hand touches the blond laminate. 'This is a desk.'

Mr Huxtable shakes his head. 'I thought you'd have a big couch and a proper desk and I'd ...'

Celia's hand touches the wooden knob. The Roll-easy drawer slides out, its passage smooth as that of a coffin's sinking to cremation. 'Look,' says Celia, shooting the drawer in and out.

Mr Huxtable nods without conviction. Celia glances at his face and straightens quickly. 'Do sit down, Mr Huxtable,' she says, demonstrating with her palm on the desk top, as though Mr Huxtable is a small animal under instruction.

Mr Huxtable lowers his arthritic hip into the grandfather chair. He drops the last few inches from stiffened knees and waits to be told what to do next.

Celia picks up her pen. 'Well, Mr Huxtable?' she says. 'How can I help you?'

Mr Huxtable drags his eyes from the invisible couch and shifts the weight from his hip.

'I'm not happy,' he says.

Celia glances up, her eyes round. What on earth's he on about?

When Celia found herself in the front seat of Rob's beat-up Escort the world leapt into sharp focus. It was the first time without Margie. The leaves of the silver poplars beside the shingle road snapped green, grey, green, grey, as the felted undersides appeared and disappeared. Rob slowed down, pulled the car onto the grass verge and switched off the ignition. One small branch was outlined against the sky. Its leaves moved and shimmered, were blotted out by his head. 'Hullo,' he said.

Mr Huxtable sits with his back to the window. Celia gives him her full attention but the butcher's shop across the road is visible over his left shoulder. The marbled reds, the rosy pinks of the different cuts are an indistinct blur, but Celia knows they lie on white plastic trays divided by inch-high fences of imitation parsley. The meat is good, the service quick, the owner Terry is obliging and will leave Celia's order with the dairy next door if she is held up, as she often is.

Margie and Rob stand side by side looking at the meat, their backs to the road. Margie's head touches Rob's shoulder for a second as she points at a tray. Their attitude, their bodies, are relaxed, connubial. They are lovers. They will choose the chops, the schnitzel, something quick, easy, and take it to Margie's flat. After Margie has driven Celia to collect the Honda she will return to the flat and they will cook the meat, eat it and fall into bed. Or before. Tonight is Rob's squash night with Des Carnihan. Margie's bright cloud of hair lifts as she turns to Rob. They enter the shop.

Mr Huxtable waits, his eyes on hers. They are old, kind, blue as her dead grandfather's. His hands nest in his lap, their skin tucked and pleated, slack and extra as lizards'.

Celia releases her fingers from the underside of the desk and presses them on top as she leans forward. There is a lull in the traffic, a screech at the lights. She stares at her patient as if he knew something important, something he could tell her. A child props a red bike against the plate-glass window opposite, balancing it with care.

Real Beach Weather

I used to be a nice woman, kind and pleasant, a dear girl once, I swear. When I was young; younger.

My husband, Derek, works in town during the week and comes to the beach only at weekends. He will be here on Friday, as the night the day. Nothing is surer. Nothing.

I, on the other hand, sit in a deck chair in the cool of the evening with Mrs Clements and her daughter who are both reasonably amiable people, especially Isobel. I am offered Twiglets, sip vodka with lime juice and tepid water and find fault in everything. I clench my fist to prevent myself shouting 'Stop talking,' at Mrs Clements, who is explaining with much detail and many diversions how she came across the vodka. She was down on her benders this morning making sure there was enough beer because if there's one thing James hates it's a drought. He is not a toper as we know, but, like all young men, he likes his beer. So there she was, head down bottom up, when lo and behold she came across this old bottle. Goodness knows where it came from. But now she comes to think of it the Parkinsons might have left it when they stayed that time before Harold died.

'Heavens above,' she cries, 'that's about, six, seven years ago. How old is Charlie now, Lorna?'

'Five.'

'Is that all? I suppose it seems longer because of his foot. Anyway, I thought we might as well try it.'

'Yes,' I say.

Warm vodka will probably be worse than warm beer but at least it will be different. It will make a change. I would like a change very much. Even the sea is boring, which I would not have thought possible. It is flat, oily, calm and predictable. The rock face of the Island beyond is stark and white as a tooth snapped from the mainland. On the seaward side of the Island, they say, are trees. Trees would be nice.

Cushioned by hillocks and dusted with sand my younger children, Ann and Charlie, loll on the couch grass in front of the verandah. They lie torpid, sated with sun and sea and glad to be here. Occasionally one of them lifts a hand in a doomed attempt to swat a fly.

The flies are bad this year, but then we say that every summer. They are large these flies, sticky-footed beach ones which cling and bite. Like children, they cannot be flicked away or ignored. Ann is now making a fuss about them, slapping arms, legs, whimpering. She has not had time to get used to them yet and will have to do so. I open my mouth to tell her so, but shut it again because I see Mrs Clements' pale eyes watching me and I don't want her to hear me being irritable. I treat Mrs Clements with respect, which is the wrong word because there are aspects of Mrs Clements which I do not, nevertheless she is a woman of great presence and I am aware of this. She is a large, well-powdered woman, not shiny with sweat like the rest of us.

Perhaps you sweat less when you are old but more probably it is because she keeps well away from the coal ranges and heated flat irons of beach life when the temperature is in the high nineties, as it has been for weeks. What are daughters for, and Mrs Clements has Isobel.

We talk about the real beach weather we have been having, we tell each other it is more comfortable in the sea than out. The nights, we say, bring little relief. The children mutter in their sleep as they toss in their bunks without a stitch of cover.

Mrs Clements says that James and Isobel were just the same at their age.

Isobel, lean and sharp-kneed, her eyes gentle behind steel rims, sits on the steps and strokes Charlie's pale hair. She has strong features like her brother who is the most handsome man in the Bay by a long shot, but a large nose and strong eyebrows are no help to Isobel. Her hair is thin and black and clamped to her head with bobby pins, not flopping in chestnut waves like James's.

Mrs Clements says yet again that this is a pity and that Isobel should have her hair permed, that she won't *try*. Isobel says No. She refuses, she likes to be free. She swims without a bathing cap, her seal head ducking and diving beneath the waves, her spectacles at home.

Charlie is now almost asleep against her angled knees. Isobel's head is bent to his. Mrs Clements hisses in my right ear, 'Poor Isobel, she's potty about that child. Of course she'll never have one of her own.' She sighs.

Some childless couples in Malaysia, I am about to tell her, adopt orphaned baby orangutans. They shave off their body hair to make them look more like human infants and dress them in appropriate clothes and are happy. I open my mouth, and, thank God, shut it again.

When I was a child my mother stressed the importance of the sorting house which, she told me, lies between the thought and the tongue. If I remembered about the sorting house I would not make gaffes like my remark at the School Sports to Arthur Smedley who was coming in last as usual – 'Come on Arthur, you'll win if you don't lose,' I cried in a loud voice *in front of everyone*.

Nowadays I have given up on the sorting house. I will say anything for a laugh and often do, but I am glad the orangutans are safely stowed.

Their story does not end there. When the orangutans are about three years old they become obstreperous and violent. Some surrogate parents hand them back to the forest rangers from whom they came, whereupon the doubly orphaned *Pongo pygmaeus* cry day and night and refuse food for weeks. Other parents abuse them or hack them to death in despair at their recalcitrant behaviour.

Mrs Clements thinks, and I know she thinks, that Isobel's fondness for Charlie is because of his foot. But I know that both Isobel and Charlie are made of sterner stuff. People stop Charlie on the beach. They ask him where he lost his foot. 'I didn't lose it,' he says. 'They cut it off.'

His left foot went the wrong way. It was all they could do.

It is essential for him to be tough and he is, thanks to me. I have made him so. Somebody had too.

I sip vodka. I have not had it before and I find it agreeable.

62

*

James Clements reappears from the back door. A small child with school sores has brought him a telephone message from the store. The Rowans up on the hill would like him to have a meal with them next Thursday. There's some cousin from Somerset and would he ring back.

James leans against the verandah post and rubs his back against it like some large and beautiful animal. He is incapable of making an ungraceful movement which is unusual in so tall a man. Even the way his heavy cotton shirt hangs from his shoulders moves me. It is James I come to watch. He is the author of the heaviness in my chest, the tightening in the groin. Even, perhaps, the clenched fist.

James is not pleased by the Rowans' invitation. 'Put on a tie and drive for miles in this heat for dog-tucker mutton! Let alone with some dim Rowan cousin. Bugger that.'

Mrs Clements smiles. Her grey curls frame her face like the frill of an antique bonnet.

'Then don't go, darling,' she murmurs.

James tells us that even the thought of trailing down to the store to tell them so makes him feel tired.

His mother is delighted at such indolence. She knows James doesn't mean it. That he will be there and back in a flash. 'Don't forget the bread order,' she laughs.

'I've done that,' says Isobel and Mrs Clements nods.

I want to tell Mrs Clements to stop being ridiculous about her son. That she is spoiling him rotten. What would she do if she had Charlie; she would ruin him, turn him into a cripple. She has already squashed Isobel, or thinks she has, but not from kindness. Mrs Clements did her best for Isobel when she was younger. She told me so herself. Take

63

the evening shoes. There were no size eights to be had then, let alone without heels. Mrs Clements bought a pair of men's leather slippers from the Farmers and Isobel painted them gold for the Ball Season.

Isobel and I met at a dinner party before the Black and White Ball, which my father called the Tight and White. Mrs Newman, our hostess, was large and golden and loved fun and games. She was an icebreaker.

I was a flapper by instinct and conviction, one of the first in the Bay to bob my hair. Straight shifts, shingled hair and high heels suited me. I was a success.

Isobel wore a long frock of some dark crêpe. Her hair was shorter than mine and better cut. She stood tall and straight and told me she wished to be elsewhere. That she had hidden the invitation, but that Mum had found the wretched thing and there had been a stink. She laughed, and watching her, I wondered at what stage slim like me becomes skinny like her. I thought she looked good. Different, certainly, from the rest of us Cuddlepots and Snugglepies, but good.

After the meal Mrs Newman gathered us together to tell us her plan for breaking the ice. The girls would each throw one shoe into the centre of the room, then sit down carefully so as to hide the still shod foot. The boys would then come in, choose a shoe and come to find its mate, thereby claiming their partner for the first dance. I was not pleased. The second best-looking man in the Bay (James had not yet returned from the War) had insisted on the first dance and I had hopes of more, many more.

We tossed shoes. Among silver pumps, louis heels, neat little brocades and pale satins, Isobel's gent's leather lay like a gilded cattle truck.

There was an embarrassed pause, a titter truncated by Isobel. She flung back her head, her short hair tossed as she laughed and laughed and laughed. I laughed too, seized her hand.

And then the men came in; and we stopped.

Mrs Clements has now given up on Isobel. For a time before she lost interest she scared the wits out of the one or two young men who hovered briefly and were never seen again. They were, she told us, unsuitable.

Sweet as a nut, I was once. Lorna Brownlee, who loved old dogs and children and was kind and patient with incontinent old men in Men's Medical.

'I'm sorry, Nurse. I done it in a fit. I'm sorry, dear.'

'Don't worry, Mr Spence,' I laughed, game as Ned Kelly with sodden sheets.

So what changed?

I had been engaged before the War, long before I met Derek, had written to my fiancé Corporal Alan Webster every week while he was overseas. The troopship berthed in Wellington and I was given special leave from the Hospital to go down to meet him. I can still hear the nagging of the train. 'What're you doing, what're you doing, what're you *doing*, you fool.' I stood on the wharf staring up at the face of the stranger beneath his lemon squeezer hat and panicked. I ran, fighting, struggling my way through the crowd pushing against me until I reached the entrance to Queen's Wharf. I arrived at the hotel, sobbing. The receptionist thought my fiancé had died en route and I wished he had, though not really.

That was when I began cheating.

A girl who jilts a wounded war hero at the moment of his triumphant return to his homeland has to start somewhere. My friend Nan said when she took off her corsets at the beach and flopped about, the sheer, physical joy of relief, the release from tension, reminded her of the first time she saw William again, alive and in one piece after the War.

Not so for me. My downhill course began with that sick scramble among the hooters and streamers and the crowds in hats waving and shouting and senseless with happiness. It was then I learned I was bad medicine. Alan Webster told me I so.

Lorna,
I cannot call you dear because you are no longer. Little did I think as I gazed at the snap I wore next to my heart all those years that you were bad medicine. I used to think that you had kept me safe. Safe for what? You are heartless and fickle. You can keep the ring. I could not take it back if you paid me.
Alan.

And I didn't mind, you see. I was glad, yea glad with all my heart to have got rid of him. Which shows there was something wrong, does it not, with both me and my heart.

I had boyfriends. Pretty girls did then, plain girls didn't, it was as simple as that. I also had a reputation. I was now flighty, if not wild. Mothers throughout the length and breadth of the Bay cautioned their sons, who took no notice. They flocked, we Charlestoned. I was fun.

I did not go to bed with these young men. They were too young, too gauche. Their hair was plastered with Brylcreem and their hot dancing hands were encased in white cotton gloves to save us from sweat marks on our dresses. Their programmes, their wee gold pencils and their groping, now gloveless hands, bored me beyond words.

The man I did love was married. We spent our time together at an hotel in Waipawa with no lift. There was a sign in the lobby saying, *Commercials Welcome.* The bottom of the dinner menu read, *Fruits in Season.*

You do not need the name of my lover. He is dead now. His shell-shocked mind caught up with him and he blew his brains out in the station woolshed not long afterwards.

I had not told him I was pregnant. What could he have done, out on the coast with his new bride and baby son and his whole life ahead of him.

Derek was slightly younger than I, and a friend of my brother's. Like Ian he had been too young for the War, a dubious privilege in the twenties. He worked in Dalgety's Stock and Station Agents and studied for his accountancy examinations at night, and had admired me from afar for years, he told me.

I smiled and said Thank you and yes, I would be happy to go with him in my new apricot cloche to the Autumn Meeting. I like racing and I sat on the steps of the Members' Stand and took covert glances at Derek's profile as he stared at the field through binoculars. He was not a bad-looking man. He had a moustache but he did not, as it were, use it much. It was just there.

He held my hand. I moved it to my knee. He glanced at me, his smile one of radiant surprise. I removed it as Mrs Cyril Bradshaw ran up the steps to tell me that people below could see my knickers, and the race began.

I knew I was pregnant. I knew what I was doing. I was

67

bad medicine. 'You must have fallen on your wedding night,' they said when my elder son Duncan was born prematurely. He was a beautiful baby. His father had been a fine-looking man.

You must understand that, like Mrs Clements, I did try. I did not love Derek Dobson but I was grateful to him. And at least I told him. 'I cannot marry you, Derek. I am pregnant. The father is dead.' I could not have made it clearer. He was shocked, deeply shocked, what young man would not have been.

But, and this perhaps is why I married him, he looked me in the eye and told me that he loved me and that if I married him he would give the child a name.

I wept. I don't think I had wept before. The baby has a name, I said, he or she has my name but not his father's because his father is dead and what about his poor little wife out at the coast, so tragic. And I meant it. It was tragic, tragic. I did nothing. It was the least I could do.

Derek, obviously, was a good man. He was also a hard worker and determined to do well. He saw his own brass plate shining before him like a vision at the end of a long uphill slog. *Derek Dobson, A.C.A.* Something he would win and lay at my feet for me to scuff.

I knew I was cheating and still do. I know.

Ann was born two years later. A solemn baby and easy after Duncan who was difficult. Babies were either easy or difficult, as girls were pretty or plain. I had to watch Duncan as a small child and still do. He is very quick.

I look around, leap to my feet. 'Where's Charlie?'

James grins at me. 'He and Isobel have gone to the store.'

'To give your message, I bet,' I say, teasing, flirting, oh the wit of it all to disguise my anger.

He smiles, nods. 'Aye,' he says. 'We all take our pleasures differently.'

And what has all this nonsense to do with me? Why do I rage inside because Isobel, who is plain, has seen fit to walk to the store to decline an invitation for her beautiful brother, who has no wish to eat tough mutton in the hills with Garth Rowan, his pigeon-toed Midge and a cousin from Home.

The Rowans for God's sake. Why should I fuss because Isobel, who has not been included in this gaiety, has acted as James' runner? She is an intelligent woman, Isobel, as well as a good sort. Besides, as James so rightly says, she will enjoy her time alone with Charlie. I see them walking in single file to the store where the beaten track through the bleached grass is thinnest, side by side where it widens. Charlie will be telling her things, he is a talker. He will be swinging himself along on his crutch, his face glancing up at hers to make sure she has got the full impact of his favourite story from his weekly comic, the one called 'Betcha Barnes and his One Wheel Wonder', which his father will bring out on Friday. He will also bring liquorice allsorts. Charlie doesn't like the black rubber ones but Annie does and she lets him eat her hundreds and thousands which fall off.

Charlie has been known to hang around outside the beach store. He leans on his crutch, his eyes sad beneath his floppy grey sunhat, which all children wear this summer because of the polio epidemic, and stares at strangers as they come out clutching Frosty Jacks or Eskimo Pies. His eyes widen as he stares at their bounty. 'Just what I like,' he

69

murmurs, and they rush back to Mr Girlingstone sweating behind the counter to get something, anything, quickly, for the waif at the door.

I checked when Duncan told me this story. I spied on Charlie and told Derek when he came out at the weekend.

'Ten out of ten for initiative,' I laughed.

I do that, you see, I do it all the time. I exaggerate my lack of moral tone so that Derek will overreact, will respond with pompous platitudes and I can laugh at him.

I stoke him up. He never lets me down.

Nor did he this time. He told me that there is initiative and initiative, called Charlie to him, sat him on his knee and explained to him that he must no longer ask people for ice creams at the store.

Charlie explained that he didn't ask for them, that people gave them to him.

Derek said he realised that technically this was so, but in actual fact Charlie was begging for them and this must stop.

Charlie said he liked ice creams.

Derek said he realised this but that Charlie was exerting moral blackmail and this must stop.

'How?' asked Charlie.

'Well, just stop.'

'No, I mean how blackmail?'

'Well you look sad and . . .' Derek waved a worried hand.

'The foot, you mean.'

'Yes, well . . .' Wretched, out of his depth, Derek sat silent.

Charlie looked thoughtful. 'Oh,' he said.

I laughed.

'Charlie, don't you see,' persisted Derek. 'We are lucky. I have a job, so many people still have no jobs, their children have no money for ice creams.'

'Annie gave one of her dolls away,' offers Charlie. 'At school.'

Derek's face, Derek's happy face. 'Did she?' he breathes. 'Did she say why?'

'The girl didn't have one. She had plaits.'

'The little girl?'

Charlie's white-blond head moves. 'The doll. Elsie.'

I bite my lip, literally bite my lip but the sorting house fails again. 'She didn't like Elsie much,' I say.

Derek's face.

Charlie is a truthful child. 'She did, Mum,' he says. 'She liked her a lot.'

Derek eyes shut briefly. He tries again. 'Yes, well. So you won't do it any more?'

'Would it be all right if you didn't have a job?'

'It would be . . . it would be more understandable.'

Charlie swings around, looks up at him. He trusts his father. 'What about the foot though?'

Derek buries his head in the curve of his son's neck. His voice is muffled. 'No,' he says, 'the foot doesn't count.'

Charlie swings off Derek's knee. He picks up his crutch, grins at Derek as he scoots out the door. 'OK,' he says.

I keep my eyes, which are damp, on the fly paper hanging from the light above the table where we eat. It is black with dead and half dead flies, one still waving.

'I lied,' I say. 'Annie did like Elsie.'

'I know,' says Derek and is silent for a moment. He stands, looks at me sadly and delivers his verdict. 'You

71

really must stop the children saying OK all the time, Lorna.'

The evening breeze stirs the tamarisk. The breakers no longer roar, their sound is muted as the waves retreat, are sucked back, return with more water. I don't believe the moon controls the tides. Waxing and waning, all that. It seems very far-fetched to me. On moonlit nights when we swim naked phosphorus sticks to our bare flesh. Phosphorus is mysterious, inexplicable as moons and tides, all that.

James lights a Craven A and hands the match to Annie to blow out. She does so but James has got it wrong. It is Charlie who enjoys blowing out matches. Ann teeters on the brink of becoming one of the big kids like Duncan, and there are things she has put aside.

The smoke rises around James's shadowed head, the light is fading. His face is all angles, hollows, manly beauty at dusk. I think of the *Indian Love Call*, 'When I'm calling you, ooh-oo, ooh-oo,' and wish to do just that. I wish Mrs Clements and Isobel would go away and I could make things clear, or perhaps clearer, to James. I am not a good woman, though presumably even a good woman may feel this clench, this awareness that her heart is beating and has been for some time. For her husband.

James leans forward, plants a hand on each knee and tells us his news. 'I'm going to make a film with my movie camera this summer,' he says. 'Cowboys and Indians, goodies and baddies, that sort of thing.'

Mrs Clements and I are impressed. Movie cameras are new in the Bay and much desired.

'Acting, you mean?' says Mrs Clements finally, as though trying out a new word.

'Yes. You can ride, can't you, Lorna?'

'Yes,' I whisper.

'We'll have to get another cowboy from somewhere and two men, both bareback riders preferably, for the bad guys. Dark sinister-looking coves.'

I inspect a loose board on the verandah. 'Isn't that a bit obvious,' I mutter.

'Cowboy flicks are obvious. That's the whole point. Their conventions are as rigid as morality plays.'

'Who wears the white hat?' I ask, knowing already.

'Me,' says James.

'Yes,' says Mrs Clements. 'But who will work the camera?'

'Bel.'

'Ah,' says Mrs Clements and re-arranges her skirt.

There will be parts for all of us; Mrs Clements will run a Wild West gambling den. There is a Madonna-of-the-plains type part for my friend Nan Lane next door.

Her husband William is Maori and can also ride bareback, which will be useful in the action scenes like the thundering chase along the surf beach.

Mrs Clements says that she'd always been interested in charades and dressing up, pretending to be somebody else, that sort of thing. She tells us she was a fairy once at school and what was James looking for? A tough egg. Well, she could try. But she wouldn't ride bareback.

She has an idea. 'James,' she says, 'do you think any of the men at the pa would be interested? William could ask them.'

James face is now in deep shadow at the back of the verandah but you can hear him smile.

'Local colour, you think?'

Mrs Clements laughs.

The tide is out on the beach below. Maori men and women dig for pipis, their children roll on the shining pewter sand. Somebody calls. The sound echoes, cuts across the car noises coming from Ann who is now pushing Dinky cars around tracks made through the rough grass.

Duncan's father told me once, and he was right, that every person in the world when shown a group photograph, looks for themselves first. Besides, I want to change the subject.

'What's my part?'

'Yours?' James looks at me as though I already knew. 'Oh, you play the bad girl. The harlot with the heart of gold.'

'How do we know,' I gasp, 'that she has a heart of gold?'

'She saves me at the end. From certain death.'

I see Mrs Clements' pale eyes on me. She is no fool, Mrs Clements.

'I'm going to find Charlie,' I cry.

But Charlie and Isobel, hand in hand and still talking, are coming through the gate past the hole for rubbish which James digs every year. No wonder there are flies.

I leap up. 'Thank you so much, Mrs Clements.'

'Hardly a party, dear, just informal drinks.'

An informal ex-peanut butter jar of warm vodka.

Mrs Clements is congratulating James. She thinks the film will be a triumph. She loves the idea of the Wild West gambling den. Does James remember the poem his father used to recite? More of a ballad really. Something about Winifred the Wonder of the West and how people said she had a hairy chest. And James has written the story himself? She shakes her head in wonder.

Isobel tells us that Yes, James has asked her to be the cameraman and she would like to. She smiles her slow smile. 'Rather fun.'

'Beat you home,' I call to the children and we scramble through the broken-down fence at the place where Charlie can slide through. I swing him upwards, hug his brown thinness, kiss his salty ear.

'Oh Charlie,' I say.

Ann and Charlie have extended the Dinky car tracks among the long creeping roots of the couch grass in front of our bach, which is next door to the Clements'. There is now a hill town and a town on the flat, garages burrow into hillsides, a hospital marked with a wilting yellow gazania indicates where you are taken when you crash. As well as the cars there is a pick-up truck, a London bus and a milk van. Each child operates three vehicles, leaving two stationary as they brrm off with the third as required. The school bus has broken down. Brrm, brrm.

The thing I like best is their concentration, their complete absorption in the realities of their invented world.

Powered by Ann, an ambulance ploughs to the scene of a major crash. Invisible men jump out.

'Is he dead?' asks Charlie.

'Nearly. This may be a case for Betcha Barnes himself.'

'Betcha,' squeaks Charlie, 'but we haven't got a One Wheel Wonder.'

'We have! Look!' Ann snaps a minute tyre from a red car. Charlie is suspicious, looks doubtfully at his plundered

Austin. Betcha Barnes is his, not Annie's. She has pinched him.

'You're not allowed. They get lost. Mum says.'

Ann's bare feet wriggle deeper in sand. She does not like interruptions. 'Do you want a One Wheel Wonder or not?'

'He's mine,' mutters Charlie.

'He can't be yours. He's in *Rainbow*. He's everybody's.' She trundles the wheel towards the yellow gazania. 'See. Now, he's rescued the man. He's all bleeding and Betcha's whizzing him to the hospital and . . .'

'No!' Charlie snatches the tyre and flings it into his mouth. He coughs violently, tears spurt from his eyes. I leap from the verandah, seize him above the knees to up-end him, beat his back. He coughs, splutters, sobs with fright as I beat and beat and beat.

'Is he going to die?' yelps Ann. The tyre shoots from Charlie's mouth.

I hold Charlie, swing him upright. I tell him it's all right, all right, it's all right.

Ann, shivering with fright and white to the bone, tells Charlie he shouldn't have put the tyre in his mouth.

'He's mine,' gasps Charlie as the Buick turns into the open gate and Derek toots the horn in greeting. He has arrived bearing basic provisions and fresh meat, beans from the garden, and treats as well. Watermelon and a tray of white-fleshed peaches from Morley's orchard, *Rainbow* and *Teddy's Own*, the week's mail and two yellow Gollancz detective stories for me.

'Charlie nearly died,' says Ann and picks up the sticky wet tyre.

Derek wants details. I give them. He takes Charlie from my shaking arms, asks him why he put the tyre in his

76

mouth. Daddy has told him a thousand times not to put things in his mouth. Charlie, limp with exhaustion, opens his eyes. 'Have you got my *Rainbow*?'

Derek tells Ann that this must be an example to her. He has told all you children not to remove the tyres from Dinky toys. They get lost and as this incident has shown they can be very dangerous, though why in the name of Heaven a big boy like Charlie should swallow a toy tyre is beyond him.

Charlie closes his eyes. Ann says how could she know Charlie was going to go all dopey and swallow it.

Derek looks at *Brave New World* lying face downwards in the sand where I must have flung it.

'Were you reading?'

'Have you any objection?'

'No, but . . . No.' He pauses, looks around. Is unhappy. 'Where's Duncan?'

'With Mike from the store.'

'Where?'

'I've no idea.'

Derek puts Charlie down. 'I think I'll have a look around first before I unpack the car.'

'Where're the sweets, Dad?' cries Ann, scrabbling in the boot of the car.

'Yeh!' cries Charlie flinging himself around Derek's suited legs. He sees the wreckage beneath the town shoes; the collapsed towns, the hospital. 'You've mucked it all up, Dad,' he wails. 'Look, all our roads, everything, all busted.'

'Sometimes,' says Derek, glancing around as though Duncan might pop up from a nearby sandhill, 'I wonder why I drive over that filthy road every Friday night and back every Sunday.'

Charlie has found his comic. He pats Derek's leg kindly. 'To bring *Rainbow*,' he tells him.

And to make love to his wife on Saturday night. Derek is a meticulous lover. Normally he rubs and squeezes and twiddles and asks me whether I like it and I say yes and I fear he does not believe me, and nor do I. But he tries. And so do I. Sometimes he asks me if I would like to try another way and I say how and he says backwards and I say no thank you as I have said many times before, so he pumps away and I help. 'Help me,' he says and I do.

But tonight is different. He is excited, perhaps, by the heat, the blackness, the slick of sweat. Union is achieved, fulfilment is given, need assuaged. I have no longing afterwards, as I sometimes do, to leap from the sagging bed and the dead mattress and rush into the still night and scream for a man, any man, to finish me off.

At home it is the milkman. At the beach it is James Clements or occasionally Chris Appleton who is a strong swimmer but leaves the water when people start fooling about beyond the breakers because why should he risk his life.

I roll over. My hand brushes Derek's back.

'Dear heart,' he murmurs. 'I do love you so.'

'Yes,' I say. 'I know.'

Balance

In that drift of time between awake and dreaming, Tommo comes back. I see the shape of his back bent over the slides, or the way his hand moved, a wave from the morgue. I haven't been back for years. It was only a temporary job.

He was still shocked when they brought him in to hospital. He could hardly speak, or wouldn't, except to tell you his name. 'Tommo,' he'd say, staring through you as though you were Perspex. He wouldn't talk about the War. How long he'd been sick. What had happened. Anything. They tried to make him, they said he was bottling things up. He must learn to verbalise to release the trauma, they said.

I never heard him verbalise. Not once, all the time he was in the ward. If they pressed him too far he'd heave himself up, bend his head as though he was getting a medal from a general and hobble away.

Every morning I'd swing the chair into the day room to collect him for his session with the consultant. Tommo would put down whichever ripped magazine he'd been stroking, then lever himself up with his stick and stand waiting. Above the collarless grey dressing-gown, the back of his pale neck was naked and vulnerable as a boy's. He had a walking plaster so he didn't really need the chair, but it made things easier. I took him to Physio in silence. I took him back to the ward. Until the day he disappeared.

I found him in the cemetery which spills down the hill behind the hospital, in terraces like in photos of Japan. He was sitting on a concrete-covered grave in his faded hospital pyjamas. The cords of hospital pyjamas are always unravelled and he was playing with them while the tears ran down his face. When he saw me he picked a handful of white marble chips from the grave. He sorted them carefully and gave me the largest.

'Thanks, Tommo.'

He wasn't violent, not ever, but it was unnerving trying to get through to him. It was worse of course for his wife June. She had shiny dark hair and she used to clutch the sleeve of my uniform and ask, 'Why's he cry all the time?' Then she would tell me how he used to laugh. He was so funny, he made everyone laugh. Everyone. Why's he cry all the time?

After a few months they thought they'd have to send Tommo down the line for specialist treatment. There was nothing much physically wrong with him now and they had given him a smaller plaster. Dr Lee disagreed. He was young and he didn't mind the tears and the patients liked him.

'Go a couple of rounds this morning, Mr Johansen?' he'd say to some old wreck on a drip, and the old man would suck his remaining teeth and say he'd come out fighting if Doctor would give him another pint like the one last night. The other patients in Men's Surgical would grin at each other, comforted.

Dr Lee must have persuaded the consultant. The best course was for Tommo to go home and cry if he wanted and no more questions. Time the great healer, said Dr Lee.

So Tommo went home to June and the baby, and Dr Lee was right again. The baby was a help. It didn't ask questions and it took up a lot of time and it laughed all over the place, especially when Tommo blew on its stomach or took it for walks in the cemetery. I used to meet them there sometimes on my way to afternoon duty. Tommo would be propped against a weathered tombstone while the baby inspected the rough grass between the graves and the pink and red valerian stirred above their heads. The baby and Tommo had the same hair. Thin and so fine it lifted in the breeze like pale silk.

If Beach the Head Porter wasn't on I'd stop for a while. Tommo talked more every time I saw him. You could see why he had a nickname. A man to pass the time of day with till dark. A yarner.

'The Catholic padre was the only one who was any use, and I'm not a Mick. "Hasta mañana, Madre, adiós," he'd say. Every night he'd say that.'

'Why, Tommo?'

'God knows. But the tomorrow sounded good.' His eyes followed the bird sideslipping the cliff above us.

'Wouldn't it be terrible to be a bum seagull?' he said.

'What?'

'No poetry of motion. Shit. And you'd starve too.'

'You'll have to get a job soon,' I said the next time I met them. Jealous. Him lying there.

Tommo picked a piece of lichen from the baby's mouth. 'Kee bor bor! Dirty. Pooh!' The baby looked at him like a blank pudding. Tommo stared up at me.

'Are there any orderlies' jobs going?' he said.

I shut up then. There was a job going, but it was a special. Mortuary porter. You need a lot of balance for that job and I didn't think balance was Tommo's strong point.

I retrieved the po-faced baby from the top of the grave and, hooking my little finger, dug a marble chip from its mouth.

'Kee bor bor,' said Tommo automatically. Still staring at me, his eyes calm.

'You'll have to ask old Beach.'

'OK.'

I didn't say anything to Beach. What could I have said? Don't take him . . . He used to cry. And I liked Tommo a lot more than that walrus-moustached sod. Every time Beach had a cup of tea he'd stir the spoon round and round and round and round. I always meant to time him. I'd feel myself sinking into the middle of the middle ring beneath the spoon. His wife used to stir his sugar in at home, he told me.

There's a curve outside Physio where the trolleys start to waltz. I met Tommo there a week later, pushing the mortuary pie-cart on his own. He was concentrating so hard he didn't see me at first. The pie-cart is really a two-man affair. It was lunchtime and the corridor was full of the crashing rattle of the ward trolleys as they lurched against each other like steel dodgems on a gleaming surface.

'You got the job then, Tommo?' I said, taking evasive action from the unattended end of the pie-cart.

Tommo kept pushing. 'Yeah.'

'This your first trip?'

'No, I was lucky the first time. I had Nick. Death's part of life,' said Tommo. 'Nick said that.'

Nick was a huge man. Even his eyelids seemed heavy as they sagged low over his eyes. His friend Theo was nimble, a quick darting performer who swirled the sacks of dirty laundry about the polished floors in sweeping curves instead of just kicking them along. Their meetings were rituals, right hands chopping down to shake the other, left hands embracing, slapping each other's backs as though they'd won again by meeting, indifferent to the currents of people streaming either side. They didn't give a stuff.

Tommo settled quickly into the routine. He was hard-working, neat and respectful to the quick and the dead, and the morgue had never looked better. The stainless steel had always gleamed but Tommo extracted an extra shine with Brillo.

The pathologist, Dr Klaus, liked him and promoted Tommo to assisting with the post-mortems. They were a good team. Tommo told me that Dr Klaus would come in, take off his lab coat, bow from the waist and put on the gear. 'If you are ready, Mr Thompson? Thank you.'

Tommo had a little workshop behind the p.m. room, which he kept as spotless as every other place in the department. The shelves were lined with bottles, beneath whose ground-glass stoppers specimens floated; some unrecognisable, some joltingly familiar. I never knew what was going to peer back at me from Tommo's shelves. His attitude to the bits and pieces was as caring as their original owners'. He was proprietorial about them too. Took a professional interest in size, shape, number. Though he wouldn't talk about where or who they came from. No gossip, nothing juicy. Jeeze, the stories he could've told

83

from that place – murder, rape, self-inflicted wounds, you name it.

I tried hard enough.

'Come on, Tommo,' I'd say, waving a jar with something pale and grey drifting about in formalin. 'What does it matter? The guy's dead now. Was he a boozer? You can tell me.'

But no. Never. He wouldn't.

Dr Klaus wouldn't have stayed in a town as small as ours if his English had been better. He taught Tommo how to prepare the specimens right up to the final staining of the slides. I used to envy the assistant as I crashed about the place, heaving and tugging and having to be cheerful to boring old buggers in pain. Tommo was always pleased to see me. I would lean against the incubator smoking, while he bent over the staining bench, the shape of his shoulder-blades visible beneath the white coat. Sometimes I'd wait for him to finish. He always left everything ready for the morning. It saved time, he said. Then we'd walk together through the cemetery, past the old house I had known as a child, down to the pub which clings by its eyebrows to the edge of the hill. Tommo and June lived further down the valley in a yellow cottage below the road.

The Lab was next door to the mortuary and the technologists liked Tommo as well. He stuck the tissue sections onto the slides with egg-white, and when necessary he would ask one of the girls to separate it from the yolk. Whichever one he asked would leap up from the bench, laughing. They all asked after the baby but it was Tommo they were talking about. As June said, he could make them laugh. Yarners can. And he could dance. At the Christmas

Dance, hot and steaming in the Nurses' Social Hall, the streamers limp and the fruit cup spiked with lab alcohol, the girls fought to dance with Tommo. One small black shoe out, gentle and slow to the beat, then swirl, his hand low on her curve and around. Oh shit, I could've killed him as their hair swung around their damp little faces and they danced. June was quite happy and the baby slept soundless in the room with the coats.

I left at the end of that summer. I called in to Tommo's room at the end of my last shift. He placed the stained slides in the incubator to dry overnight then washed his hands, slipping the green soap from palm to palm. The overhead light shone directly on his head and I could see the pink scalp beneath the pale hair. He locked up and we walked down through the cemetery past the old house on the corner.

The old house had been beautiful once. Lack of paint had leached the walls to silver and the whole place shimmered in the late afternoon heat, outlined against dark macrocarpas. I had played on that sagging verandah, my nose level with the lowest streams of nutmeg-scented wistaria. Terror had stained the ground beneath those trees when I'd trodden on a rusty old coil of wire and it had struck my leg like a snake in fury.

The owner had sold the house to a small silent widow named Mrs Wellers. The house settled down around her, still and quiet as its new owner.

She had been found dead that week, slumped on the verandah in her nightdress, the bleached boards cool beneath her.

There had been an inquest of course, and a police post-mortem. A reporter had attempted to interview Dr Klaus.

85

He escorted the young man to the door, asking in his careful English, 'Is nothing sacred in this country?'

'Did her post-mortem show anything suspicious, Tommo?' I said as we passed. 'You know? Violence or anything?'

Tommo glanced at me. 'God, you're a weirdo,' he said, and ran down the steep path.

One of the things I like best about a pub, especially that one, is the first surge of light and sound as you push open the door. Shouts and laughter splintered to the roof and echoed back from the barman's armoury of glass and light.

'I'll get them,' I said, shoving forward to the bar.

I carried the glasses high, working a path back to Tommo through the curses and spills.

'Here, Tommo.' He took the glass and stared into it as though he could see something in it other than the beer which sloshed over the side as someone knocked his arm.

There was a long silence, I remember, then I said, 'You know something, Tommo? I don't reckon I could do your job.'

Tommo lifted his eyes from his glass and stared at me as though I was something uprooted from the tartan carpet.

'No,' he said. 'You couldn't. And I'll tell you why you couldn't. Because death's a part of life, and you've got no respect for either.'

Then he put down his glass and turned to the door. The window was open, there was a breeze from the sea. Above the roar of the bar noise I could hear his feet clattering down the concrete steps as he ran.

The Grateful Dead

First thing I remember knowing was not some lonesome whistle blowing or a young 'un's dream of growing up to ride. First thing I remember knowing was that my father liked my mother a lot but my mother didn't like my father. Hardly at all, not even at Christmas.

'Not another stupid vase,' she muttered, poking a stiff finger at a large vase-shaped parcel wrapped in red and green paper with reindeer.

I put my hand on her knee. 'This one'll be nice, Mum,' I said. 'Truly.'

'Huh,' said my mother and left the room. I stroked the parcel, put it down carefully.

'You're a lucky girl, you've got the prettiest Mum in town,' the butcher told me, the liver in his hand bleeding tears of blood onto the sawdust beneath. He slammed an inadequate piece of paper onto the scales, laid the liver to rest and peered at the reading. Both hands stroked the skirt of his striped apron, leaving tracks.

'Wouldn't mind being a number two then, Fred?' enquired the baker, who had popped in from next door for a bit of shin on the bone.

Fred grinned at the baker and winked at me to show that the baker was a caution and I mustn't mind. I didn't. Like much in life, the baker was inexplicable.

I imagined the butcher choosing his weekend joint with care; furrowed brow, lips pursed, pork fingers clutching the edge of the chilled display cabinet as he leant over to choose from the red rounds of beef, the forequarters of lamb, the legs. How did he recognise the very best one of all? Even better, presumably, than the one he saved each week for my mother. Marbled flesh I knew about, but what were the other signs of grace?

'Are you going to be as pretty as your Mum when you grow up?' asked the man who made Christmas candles in his shed at the back of his section. I had called in for some gold ones on the way home. I laughed once more to show I knew it was a joke and didn't mind, but I was full of doubts.

My father was interested in grammar. He said I didn't have any. He sat at one end of the table and told me not to say 'got'. 'I *have* ten biscuits, not I have *got* ten biscuits.'

I was allowed only one biscuit but knew the fact was irrelevant.

My mother sat at the other end of the table and said nothing. Her hair was coiled around her head. There was not a hair out of place.

'Your mother never has a hair out of place,' marvelled the ladies in the town.

'I know,' I said with pride. I watched her doing it. Brushing and brushing then both hands snatching to twist slam bang and stick with pins as though she hated it.

I longed for plaits. 'Please, Mum, please.'

My mother said no. Plaits were untidy. They came undone.

I put posies of rosebuds and gypsophila on her dressing-table all summer. I was good at posies. I won a prize in the Children's Section at the Agricultural and Pastoral Show. My daisies and cornflowers with red geraniums for contrast sat in a regulation vase in the Produce Shed alongside a stiff yellow card. Highly Commended, it said.

My father played bowls. Bowls made him happy, even the thought of bowls made him smile. He forgot about 'got' on Saturdays and strode down the concrete drive in long white trousers and white shirt and white shoes with no heels because of the turf surface, his bowls in a domed case and gladness in his heart.

He met Mr Duras at the Bowling Club and brought him home. Mr Duras was hail-fellow-well-met. He said so himself, in our living-room.

'Call me D,' he said, holding out arms which I avoided.

How could I call him D? He was grown-up and unknown. And how did you spell it?

Mr Duras made jokes and my mother and father laughed as the late-afternoon sun fell through the plane trees and warmed their backs.

'Shall we have a drink?' said my father, looking at my mother to see if it was all right. My mother nodded. Not a hair moved.

Mr Duras sprang to his feet. 'Good thinking,' he cried. 'Let me help you, Douglas. Can I call you Doug? Let me help.'

'No, no,' said my father. 'You keep Ella happy.'

My father asked Mr Duras and my mother what they

89

would like to drink and Mr Duras looked happier than ever and said, 'Brandy, thanks, Douggie. And ginger ale.'

My mother said she would have one too, why not, and I sat on the floor and coloured in the pictures in Flower Fairies of the Spring with my crayons because my mother said I could. I never went over the edge, even when doing the hard bits, like eyes. I was very careful.

Mr Duras came after Bowls and sometimes during the week. He gave my father lifts to Bowls and then had to bring him back. 'Beauty,' said Mr Duras as he slammed the door shut on my father's side and ran round to his side of the De Soto. 'Beauty.' My father called Mr Duras Mr Beauty for a joke, but my mother didn't laugh and my father stopped.

I ran up the hill to my grandfather's, an over-sized Little Red Riding Hood bearing gifts. I took bits of pudding in plastic bowls with frilled plastic hats to stop them spilling, left-over bits of casserole, slices of meat on a covered plate. All these I took in a flat basket so they wouldn't spill. If the puddings were sloshy I walked.

The smell of lysol was evident long before you saw the monkeys in their cage at the Zoological Gardens next to the men's lavatory. The monkeys took no notice of me and my basket. They were small with bright pink behinds and they curled side by side and hid their eyes behind their arms when they were not leaping about shrieking, or hunting for fleas in one another's fur with long snapping fingers.

'It'd be a million times easier if he'd live with us,' my mother told people about her father. 'All this endless ferrying of food. There's plenty of room but he won't. You know what they're like,' said my mother.

My grandfather played Harry Lauder records on his old wind-up gramophone and laughed till he cried. 'Stop y' tickling, tickle ickle ickling. Stop y' tickling, Jock,' piped Harry Lauder, as the tears ran down my grandfather's face.

'Won't you come and live with us, Grandad?' I begged. 'Please.'

He shook his head and reached for his smelly old pipe from the ashtray with shells on it. 'Not likely,' he said. 'Not likely, sweetheart.'

I stopped on the way home to check on a small white magnolia in a park near our house. I liked the thick torn-paper petals, the furry grey of the tight buds, the heavy scent.

Mr Duras was sitting by himself on a wooden seat beside the bush.

'Hullo, D,' I said, proud of my casual use of Mr Duras's Christian name, if it was.

A bud brushed the brim of Mr Duras's hat as he jumped.

'Hullo,' he said.

'What are you doing here?'

Mr Duras coughed. 'I like these things' smell,' he said.

Perhaps I had got Mr Duras wrong. I sat down beside him. He took my hand. I removed it.

'Don't say anything about seeing me here to your Dad, will you, girlie?'

'Why not?'

'It's our little secret. You like secrets, I bet. All little girls

91

like secrets,' said Mr Duras, jumping about on his bottom with excitement.

I hated secrets. Secrets were exclusion.

'All right.' I stood up. 'I've got to go now, Mr Duras.'

He nodded. 'Don't forget,' he called after me as I belted home with my empty basket.

Mr Duras appeared as usual on Saturday to pick up my father. We had had a scratch lunch, my mother called it. Cold meat and pickles and bread because she had been making chutney all morning and had had it up to here with food. The house sang with the scent of spices.

'Pickle factory,' snorted my mother.

She was standing halfway up a small step-ladder, stowing the full jars away when Mr Duras arrived. 'Beauty,' he said, clapping his hands as he often did when he said it. 'Beauty.'

My mother's smile, even to Mr Duras, was brief. 'And who's going to hand them up?' she said, snatching a warm shining jar of peach chutney from my father's outstretched hand.

'I will, Mum,' I cried, pink with excitement at the thought.

My mother laughed. I had been known to drop things.

My father looked miserable.

Mr Duras knew my father had a needle match at two. He had a solution. He saw it in a flash. He handed his car keys to my father. 'Take the De Soto, Douggie,' cried Mr Duras. 'I'll walk round when I've handed up this lot. Do me good, lovely day. Lovely.'

'No, no, no,' said my father. 'I'll take the Dodge, but if you could give Ella a hand with this lot, that'd be grand.' He slapped Mr Duras on the shoulder. 'Thanks, D.'

'Byebye, darling,' he said.

'Goodbye,' said my mother.

I watched my father out the window. He ran, almost skipped down the drive, the domed bag swinging in his hand. 'Bye,' he called again.

Mr Duras and my mother were silent. My mother smiled down at Mr Duras, whose hand was sliding gently down her leg.

Day Out

About three times a year my friend Ruth and I drive over the Rimutaka Hill to see our friend Lindsay, who lives in the Wairarapa. We would like to make it more often and so would Lindsay, she says, but you would be surprised to find how difficult it is to get three women organised for the same day, same time, weather permitting.

This is because we are busy. We are not proud of this fact. When people ask us how we are we do not reply, 'Busy.' Busy is not how you are. Busy is what you do with days.

Nevertheless, we are.

One of the reasons Ruth is busy is because she and Tom are good grandparents and either she is visiting grand-children to the North, or the South, or locally, or they are coming to stay.

Ruth and Tom like this and know how lucky they are. Ruth is also an ace cook and hospitable as well. Twenty-four for Christmas dinner, you know the type. Her daughter cooked the turkey this year. But even so.

Ruth also does good by stealth and is funny with it.

When I say weather permitting, I mean it. Who would

94

want to drive over that hill in a gale? I don't enjoy it in fair weather with a following wind, but Ruth likes driving, which is lucky for me. I'm not bad at the wheel, I have never had an accident but don't quote me. It's just that either you're keen or you're not. I've never been a bags-I-drive kind of girl. Or indeed bags-I-anything much.

Our friend Lindsay is also a busy woman. She cooks and sews and reaps and hoes and her husband, John, is not getting any younger. Lindsay also has grandchildren; older, busier, coming and going they frequent her days. Her daughters are busy too. Astonishingly busy. Lindsay doesn't know how they do it, and nor do I. Most people in the Wairarapa are busy. There is not much ambling or rambling: except, of course, on the Wine Trail.

Ruth tucks two or three cushions underneath her so she can see over the wheel, and we're away. We cruise along beside the Hutt River. We note the debris from the last flood, the broken branches, the silt piled against the willow trunks. Goodness, we say. We talk all through Upper Hutt, which, as always, goes on for longer than you would expect. We sail over the first group of small hills which are a preliminary hurdle before the five-bar of the Rimutaka itself.

I realise I am exaggerating. There's nothing wrong with the Rimutaka Hill and it's better than it was. I know a young woman who drives a twenty-six-wheel articulated truck over it twice a day and loves every minute. During the First World War when the men had finished their training in Featherston they marched, in full kit, up and over the Rimutakas to Wellington.

Nevertheless, I still don't like it. It is covered in bush and scrub. 'Its cliffs are sombre and its defiles mysterious,' but the road is too near to both.

Ruth is unperturbed. Before long we are up and over, have passed through Featherston which is the Gateway to the Wairarapa and are creaming down the straights towards Masterton. The power lines are singing along beside us and we are still talking.

To our left lie the mountains, but Ruth can only glance. Shadowed with clouds and wreathed in mist, their leviathan shapes of blue, grey and purple roll on forever. They are mysterious and unknown, and likely to remain so.

We agree with the psalmist who wrote, 'I will lift up mine eyes unto the hills, from whence cometh my help.' We nod our heads in unison. However, we are not convinced that our help cometh from the Lord, let alone that He made Heaven and Earth.

Ruth adjusts one of her cushions with a quick heave and says that if the help which cometh from the hills doesn't come from the Lord, where does it come from? That we can't have it both ways.

I say that's not the point. We can get a sense of numinous awe from the sublime wonders of Nature without . . .

'What's numinous?'

'Spiritual, awe-inspiring.'

'Like God.'

'Well, a local deity, perhaps. Small g.'

'Like the Maoris?'

'No, but . . .' I see the sign in the nick of time. 'Mushrooms!' I shout, and we turn onto the side road and head for the farm.

'How do you feel,' I say later when we get back to

Ruth's car with our five-dollar trays of mushrooms and what good value, 'how do you feel about us lending fifty-seven million dollars to help bail out the financially embattled South Korean Goverment?'

Ruth resettles a large, fresh, pink-gilled mushroom. Mushrooms are fragile and she does not want any to spill or spoil before we get home. She gives a smaller darker one a reassuring pat before getting back into the driver's seat. She snaps her safety belt, plumps her cushions. 'I can see why it makes sense,' she says. '"Major New Zealand trading partner, fifth largest market, vested interest in its recovery." All that. But ...'

'The Minister of Finance says that the chances of getting the loan back are "very high".'

'"Very high,"' says Ruth, 'is not high enough.'

We are silent as we drive through Carterton, which goes on longer than the previous village, Greytown. One is considered more desirable than the other but I can never remember which.

'The Accident and Emergency Department,' says Ruth suddenly, 'is so run down there are holes in the linoleum.'

'I know.'

'However, my main problem at the moment,' she says after a pause, 'is my funeral.'

I give her profile one startled glance, then calm down. Ruth, her eyes focused on the road ahead, is not thinking about the immediate future. Ruth is onto abstracts, the practicalities of these abstracts are giving her concern.

'In what way?'

'You *know*,' Ruth says you *know* quite often, and pokes you for emphasis, though not at the moment. 'Being

Jewish, going to an Anglican boarding school, marrying a Welshman. I feel I've lost my *roots*.'

I take a quick peek over my shoulder to check the mushrooms. 'What's that got to do with your funeral?'

'Everything,' says Ruth. 'Who's going to *do* it?'

'You don't have to have anyone now. Not a professional. You can get a co-ordinator. A sort of MC.'

'Who?' says Ruth, staring sourly at the straight black asphalt unrolling before her and not another soul in sight.

'Anyone. A family friend. Marriage celebrant. Some vicars don't mind no God now.'

'But which *sort* of vicar.'

'What about a rabbi?'

Her glance withers. 'I don't belong to the Jewish faith. I never have. How can I start at this stage?'

'You could read it up.'

'*Read it up.*'

I know what she means. I had a T-shirt once. *So many books, so little time.*

'And anyway,' she says. 'I don't know that I want to.'

'Then why fuss?'

Ruth sighs. 'There're some peppermints,' she says, 'in the glove box.'

They are large peppermints, dusted with soft sugar; good of their kind, but cumbersome.

We take one each, suck in silence. 'It's because,' she says eventually, 'I'm scared of death,'

'I can't see for the life of me how the sort of funeral you have is going to help that,' I say. 'You're putting the cart before the horse.'

'Well, they'll have to do something,' she says. 'Won't they?'

'Yes, but why should it worry *you*? You'll be the last person on earth to be taking an interest.'

'It's all very well for you,' says Ruth.

This is true. As with everything, death only matters if you care. I am rather a chucklehead in this regard, but again, don't quote me. I try harder.

'How about the Salvation Army?' I say. 'You've always been a great supporter.'

'You can't just bail up a uniformed officer and ask him or her to take over your funeral. You're no *help*.'

'Well, then, try your local talent. The clergy.'

'I don't even know who they are.'

'Then find out. Patti, you know Patti?'

'Yes, indeed.'

'She tracked one down. Nice man. Quite young. She asked him round for a cup of tea, explained her position frankly and asked him if he would be prepared to take her funeral service at a later date. He said certainly, that was his job, or one of them, and that it would be a pleasure, or words to that effect. They had quite a merry time, Patti said, working things out, choosing this and that, getting the whole thing teed up and a rough draft down on paper, and then he had a sherry and a few nuts and departed. Patti was delighted, so pleased to have the whole thing organised. It had been hanging over her, she said.'

Ruth laughs and laughs. 'You have to hand it to Patti.'

'Yes. Except the poor man dropped dead next week.'

'How *terrible*. What?'

'Coronary.'

'So then what?'

'I'm not sure. I think Patti sort of lost heart.'

'Tt,' says Ruth. 'What a dreadful story.'

'Yes.' We are silent for a moment or two.

'I don't like those ones, do you,' I say, 'when the congregation are invited to come up and share their own memories of dear old Ralph?'

'Not much. Not when they talk to the box.'

'You can see why, though. It's all a matter of personal preference.'

'Yes,' says Ruth bleakly.

I have been tactless. 'You'll be all right,' I say quickly. 'Why don't you have one of those no-God ones and a family friend co-ordinating and a few people asked to speak. And beautiful music. You're musical. Some of those ones are lovely. You could decide the music now. That'd be something done.'

'So could you.'

'No. The *Cow Cow Boogie* wouldn't get me anywhere.' I think about it for a while then perk up. 'There's the hymns though. And those wonderful old prayers, psalms, the old words. Glorious. Restore your faith in anything. You can't beat them, really. I've been to some inspirational funerals with God and hymns and the old words.'

Ruth turns into Lindsay's carport and switches off the ignition.

'But *which* God?' she snaps.

Lindsay comes to greet us. She is pleased to see us and vice versa. She declines mushrooms. No, no. She can get them anytime. She stands beside Ruth and tells me she is half an inch taller than her, though this is a moot point.

If you boiled the three of us down you would get three average-sized women happy to be together again.

'What've you been talking about?' says Lindsay as we

walk into her house which is filled with light and warmth and welcome.

'We've been working,' I say, 'on our funerals.'

'Oh good,' says Lindsay. 'Where've you got to? Which sort? Let's have a glass of wine.'

Ruth shakes her head. 'Not for me, thank you,' she says sadly. 'I'm driving.'

Glorious Things

Autumn. No doubt about it. Dew on the grass, nip in the air. Pale sun.

Clive Harper sniffed the sparkling air. He liked autumn. It had a certainty about it which pleased him. You knew what would happen next. The stroll down the concrete path to the letterbox, the knowledge that the milk would be in the billy, the paper alongside, all pleased him.

The milkman was reliable. Very. And the paper boy.

Clutching his goods in one hand, Clive turned to a dazzle of reflected light. A burnished brass garden tap flashed back at him from the hydrangea bed. Why the hell did she polish that? He was used to things gleaming inside the house, to wood and linoleum shined to mirror surfaces. Now his mother's obsession with buffing up seemed to have moved outdoors. He glared at the thing; banged the paper against his thigh with quick irritated whacks. She would have had to force her overalled bust (*Fadeless florals, 4s.11d. Variety bewildering*) through waves of mop-headed blooms to reach the thing, apply polish and then, grunting with effort, remove the stuff and back out. There was no room to turn. If she believed in an all-seeing God he could

102

understand it. (*I shine for Thee.*) But she didn't, not a word of it, though she loved the hymns.

'*For all the saints,*' she'd bellowed in her cracked contralto that morning after dumping his Cremoata in front of him, '*who from their labours rest.* You can just see them, can't you! Lined up in rows. Serried, that's what they call them, serried rows.'

Her tongue flicked her upper lip, her hands crashed down on the yellow-toothed old Bently and she was off again – singing her heart out, giving it wings while Clive went for the paper.

'Hand us the ads, boy,' she called, heaving herself up from the Bently. '*Don't let Mrs Next Door sniff in your kitchen. Use Airwick . . . Avoid shoe shame. Use Nugget.* What do they think we are! And look at this one. *The acid in your stomach would burn a hole in the carpet.* There's even a picture. See the wee hole?' She sucked her teeth with delight at the find.

He could never work her out. Never reconcile her passion for making anything shine that could shine, for hunting dirt like a beagle on scent, for rubbing things and scrubbing things, with her total lack of concern for what anyone else in the world thought or did or said. She had no hesitancy, no apprehension. Mothers were meant to work you out, to understand you, but she'd never bothered to do that. He existed, he was there; a man going on thirty-three with slicked-back hair and crooked teeth, a two-pack-a-day man who didn't say much. What was there to say? He'd given up begging for reassurance long ago.

'Do I look all right, Mum?' he said, his hands sweating with fright before the Sixth Form Social.

His mother flapped her arm in dismissal. 'Of course you

look all right. You've got two arms, two legs, a nose. Off you go. And leave the billy in the letterbox.'

Clive had begun training as a motor mechanic when he left school, under the personal supervision of Jas Henry (*Moderate charges, Carlyle St Petrol Station*). He gave it up when he developed sore knees from kneeling on the concrete all day. He had been lucky to find a job in the china department of the Farmers' Co-Op.

His mother had been unimpressed by the change. 'You could have got a cushion,' she said, peering vaguely around the dining-room. A heavy oak sideboard supported a blue-and-white biscuit barrel, an equally empty fruit bowl and a pair of electroplated candlesticks from which the silver had long since been polished. Framed in gilt, Napoleon on horseback reared above. Clive had been disappointed to discover others had it too. He thought his hero was his alone.

A red plush cloth edged with bobbles covered the table; yellow camels trekked across red velvet cushions brought home from Cairo years ago by Clive's father, a gaunt wreck of a man who lay about for ten years after Gallipoli and then died. 'The Harpers are like the potato family,' said his widow. 'The best of them are under the ground.'

Nothing in the house was ever altered or discarded. Even the well-wiped aspidistra in its brass pot had belonged to his grandmother. His mother didn't care what anything looked like as long as she could clean it.

There was a lot of reading in the *Clarion*. Even the headlines took him quite a time. *Hitler at War with Pope.* The Pope kept the names of persecuted Catholic youths in a

White Book in the Vatican and had remonstrated with the Führer.

Where is Jardine? The question was intriguing India. Was the MCC Captain still tiger-shooting? Ten days ago he had shot an old tiger in the Mysore district, told a relative he was after a better specimen, and disappeared into the jungle.

There was a photograph, but not of Jardine. A local landowner had recently shot his second bull moose in Dusky Sound.

Clive turned the page. His hands tightened. Mary Boyle was advertising. *Miss Boyle. Dressmaker, Costumier, specialising in matrons and outsizes, hem-stitching 4d. Upstairs, Farmers' Bldgs.* There had been no money left, everyone knew that, after her father had drunk himself into the grave. Sometimes Mary had come to help him home from the Criterion at six o'clock. Jenson, the bull-necked proprietor, would telephone her. 'Sorry, Miss.' Clive had seen her a couple of times from the window. She stood calmly by the door, seemingly unconcerned by the uproar within, her face blank as she waited to prop her father on her girl's bike with its skirt-shield, and wheel him home. Clive had hidden behind his paper. He could have helped her. He should have helped her. He'd known her since primary school, since she was tiny. She was still a slip of a girl, five feet at the most, and here she was specialising in Matrons and Outsizes. More money perhaps. Clive reached for his smokes.

'Tennis on Sunday?' called Dr York, from across the hedge. Clive liked his neighbour. Dr York was an amiable man. He was large and cheerful and specialised in

105

obstetrics. He had brought Clive into the world at Sister Fahey's Nursing Home. His mother had given him details: the gas heater hissing, the nightie and booties laid out warming. 'Right in the labour room. I mean. It gave me quite a turn.'

'The usual four?' continued Dr York.

'I wondered . . .' said Clive.

'Yes?' Was the poor man blushing?

'I wondered if I could ask one or two ladies, say.'

'Ladies?' Dr York snapped an escallonia twig between his thumb and forefinger and gazed at its small red flowers.

'We, well, that is, you, could ask the White girls and Mary Boyle.'

Forceps delivery, thought Dr York automatically. The baby's head had been a real mess at the time.

'Arthur Boyle's daughter?' he said. Comment on Arthur Boyle, even in the deceased state, was not easy.

Clive nodded. 'I believe,' he said, the tide of red still surging up his neck, 'that she plays a very good game. In fact, I know she does. She was runner-up in the mixed doubles at Tikokino.'

'Ah.' Dr York squeezed a leaf, sniffed the aromatic sharpness on his fingers. 'You'll have to ask her,' he said. 'Them.'

Clive's adam's apple rose and fell. 'Yes,' he said. 'Yes. I will.'

Mrs York watched from her kitchen window as Clive adjusted his bike clips at the gate. 'Poor Clive,' she said. 'There's always been something, I don't know . . . something sort of, you know, squiffy about him.'

'Clive's all right,' said her husband, wishing they could

have hot milk with their breakfast coffee like he'd had at the base hospital in France. Mrs York said it wasn't worth the effort. It boiled over in a flash and she had better things to do.

'You think everyone's all right.'

Dr York unfolded the paper. 'He's a little . . .' Dr York waved a large hand. He didn't know what he meant himself. Shy, perhaps? More than that.

'He's all right,' he said again and changed the subject. *Renew that graceful figure,* he read aloud. *Naturettes, the non-fasting, non-exercising and safe way to reduce superfluous flesh will make today's form-fitting frocks a realisation for you. Naturettes dissolve the flesh and improve health. 17 days' treatment 7/6. Money-back guarantee.* Dr York snorted. 'Now that's something I do know what I think about.'

'I'm thinking of asking Mary Boyle to play tennis on Sunday,' Clive said, putting out a hand to the upturned cup which was skidding around on soap bubbles. 'And the White girls.'

'You've taken my leaner.'

Clive replaced the cup. 'Sorry.'

Mrs Harper leant a saucer on it. It fell off and lay flat, bubbles frothing around its rim. She stared at it. 'See that? That's the sort of thing that makes me not believe in God. What's the point in that happening? If there's a God, there's meant to be a reason for everything, isn't there?' She glared at Clive above her steamed-up glasses. 'Hairs on the head numbered, things of that nature?'

'Not for physics and stuff. Not for surface tension.' Clive knew he was on shaky ground. He'd never done physics or surface tension. He just wanted to shut her up.

107

'Surface tension,' she murmured. 'Is that right? Surface tension. I'll remember that.'

'On Sunday,' said Clive, 'I'm going to ask Mary Boyle and the White girls. For tennis at Dr York's.'

Mrs Harper flipped the end of her nose with her newly dried hand. 'Why?'

It was always the same. Always. He heard his voice. 'I thought it would be, you know . . . Nice.'

'You'd better put citric acid on the order then,' she said. 'There's no lemon drink.'

Clive left the order at the grocery section of the Farmers' Co-Op next morning. The wide wooden counter stretched the width of the shop. Behind it, white-aproned assistants were ranked in strict hierarchical order. Ken Bates, the manager, was on the left; the most junior lad far away in the shadows beside the storeroom on the right. Ken was one of Dr York's regular tennis four and had put in a word for Clive at the china department. A fine player and good at his job, he was considered to be on his way up. He was pleasant and efficient as he sliced and weighed and wrapped with speed. And popular. A bright-eyed, recently married charmer. The local farmers' wives, perched on long-legged chairs across the counter, were flattered by his attentions, his cheery grin. 'Basics first, shall we, Mrs C? Flour? How're you going on flour? Butter? Why not? Make it five, shall we? Six? Right, you're the doctor.' He slapped a hand against the dark hide of the rolled loin in the slicer beside him. 'And bacon? Lovely piece, this one. Lovely.'

The china department was less fun. Clive spent a lot of time dusting crystal bowls, Dresden ballerinas standing on one toe and mugs with rabbits selling parsnip wine. He didn't see how he could ever get on in china. Miss Kirten, the supervisor, was lean and tough and obviously would live for ever. It worried him.

He jumped slightly as a customer shoved a cut-glass decanter under his nose. 'Sorry, Mrs Stevenson. Oh yes, certainly. For the Crayford wedding, was it? Yes, of course. I'll wrap it straight away.' Clive took a deep breath. 'If you were going up to the tearooms, I could bring it up. Save you waiting and that.'

Mrs Stevenson looked at him, trying to put her finger on it. Straight-backed, a polite young man, but . . . A light flicked inside her grey head. She almost told him. Young man, you are too aware of yourself. Real men, she could have told him, don't notice themselves. 'No, thank you,' she said, tugging on a glove. 'I'll wait.'

'Right you are, then.' He had hoped to slip upstairs with the thing and knock on Mary Boyle's door on the way down. He couldn't ring from work and the telephone was beside the piano at home. Last night Mrs Harper had got stuck for hours on 'Glorious Things of Thee Are Spoken'.

'That's it then, Clive,' said Miss Kirten at five-forty. 'See you tomorrow.'

He grabbed his bike clips from the hook beside the till, ducked out the back way through hardware, dodged the buyer with a neat sidestep and ran up the steep stairs to the offices above. The pseudo-marble clattered beneath his toe plates. His hand flicked the Greek key pattern of the dado. The Farmers' Co-op had been built to last.

He stood panting outside the door. It was unmarked except for a small card, 'Mary Boyle, Seamstress'. She probably couldn't afford a gold-lettered job. Clive knocked. There was a pause. He knocked again. Mary appeared, her dark hair held back by a velvet band, her small face startled. 'What is it, Clive?'

'Can you play tennis at Dr York's on Sunday?'

'What?'

'Would you like to?'

She shut the door and stood beside him in the corridor, her face smiling. She had something exciting to tell him. 'I've got Mrs Earnshaw in there,' she whispered, jerking her head towards the door.

'Oh,' said Clive. He knew Mrs Earnshaw by sight. She often sat overflowing the chair opposite Ken Bates. Mr Earnshaw's acres were broad. He was a racing man and his brood mares were renowned.

'So I'll have to go.' Her brown eyes were sparkling. For him? For her client? 'Fifteen minutes?' she said. 'Downstairs?'

'OK.'

Clive waited outside the office exit. He sat slouched over the handlebars, one foot on the pavement, the other in the gutter. A man waiting for his girl after work. His girlfriend.

Mary came running down the stairs. 'Fancy me having Mrs *Earn*shaw! She's ordered a wool georgette for spring. From *me*.' Her feet skipped on the dusty pavement, triumphant as a child after her first high dive.

Clive beamed at her. 'Good on you.'

'You know what?'

He shook his head.

Her eyes were snapping, sparking with her secret. The impact of the tennis invitation, if it had ever existed, had disappeared. Her voice dropped as she glanced over her shoulder, checking for eavesdroppers.

'She says if the wool georgette's any good she'll tell all her friends. Mrs *Earnshaw*.'

'It will be,' he said.

She frowned slightly. 'Don't tell anyone.'

He shook his head again.

She snatched off her hair ribbon to retie it. The Farmers' corner caught every breath of wind. Dark hair blew across her face. She tugged it back with both hands. 'Don't,' said Clive. 'Leave it!'

She glanced at him, shy once more. 'What time on Sunday?'

'Two o'clock.'

'OK then. Thanks. I'd like to.' She turned to go.

'Have you got your bike?' asked Clive.

'Of course.'

'I could wait. Ride home with you.'

'But I'm way up Pakowhai Road.'

'I know.'

'Oh. Oh,' she said again. 'All right.'

They said little on the way home, the wind in their teeth, her hair all over the place. Clive could feel his heart, knew where the thump was located.

He clutched the sagging gatepost of the old villa where she lived alone. 'See you on Sunday, then.'

'Yes.'

He lifted one hand. 'See you.'

'Glorious things of *thee* are spoken, *Zion*, city of our God,' he yelled to the tossing wind on his way home. The words flew upwards, disappeared beyond the line of poplars.

Mrs Harper dumped a large yellow jug on a rickety table beneath the phoenix palms next door and departed.

111

Mrs York, after vague welcoming gestures towards Mary and Babs and Muriel White, had also disappeared. She had views about silly old buffers bounding about with bare knees.

'Ken's not bald. Or Clive,' muttered her husband.

'Clive might as well be.'

Tim Bartlett, the chemist, and Ken Bates were happy to be invited to play at Dr York's. The court had a good surface and Clive did all the work, mowing and rolling and trundling along behind the little white marking cart.

But there was no hostess, no other woman to sit with the spare girl during mixed doubles. No one to ease the strain for Babs and Muriel and the specialist in outsizes when the men's four bounded about within cooee of apoplexy, the sweat running below the white flannel bands around their scarlet foreheads.

The tennis was good. Inspired even, in patches. Babs and Muriel were not bad at all and Mary's classic style was pretty to watch. She wore a white pleated skirt, her ankle socks were white, her knees pink. Her fuji silk blouse came out from her skirt as she flung the ball a yard above her head and slammed the racquet down at the right moment. Her forehand was deep and true, her backhand not so good. Clive watched, absorbed by her every move. She became pinker and pinker, happier and happier, dancing around beside the White girls, who were good sports and known to be so.

'Tea,' called Mrs York. It was served in the dining-room and was always the same. Sandwiches which leaked tomato or cucumber and Mother's cut-and-come-again sultana cake.

The players were happy, relaxed, reached for more cake and thanked Mrs York's departing back. Clive looked at them all fondly. I, he thought, am entertaining. I am entertaining girls. He straightened his shoulders, reached for Mary's hand beneath the table cover. She edged away. Ken Bates smiled down at her. 'About your backhand, Mary,' he said.

'I know,' she murmured, gazing up at him in sorrow, 'it's terrible.'

'I could fix it in half an hour.'

'*Could* you?'

Mary wouldn't stay after tea. 'I've got to do Mrs Earnshaw's buttonholes,' she told Dr York, her eyes troubled. 'Bound buttonholes. She insists on them, even for little wee fiddly . . .' She shook her head. 'And it frays too, wool georgette.'

Clive said nothing. He could think of no word of comfort.

He wheeled her bike to the gate. 'Well,' he said.

She put out her hand. 'Thank you. I know it was you, really.'

The small hand lay in his. The formal gesture dismayed him. They'd got further than that. Hadn't they?

Husband and Wife's Handbook by *Dr Hector Cole*, he read. *A concise treatise on a subject of vital importance to married persons and those intending to marry, together with our book on Appliances Free.*

His mother toiled in from the kitchen, bearing sliced tongue.

Clive sat very still, the newspaper hiding his crotch, his face tense. 'In a minute,' he said.

'Now!' His mother waved her free arm. 'There's flies.'

Oh, God. 'In a *minute*, I said.'

Her face was the same pink-purple as the tongue. 'What's up?'

'Nothing! Nothing.'

She put the plate on the table and slid into her chair, both hands flat on the table for support. 'Well, then,' she said, the serving fork poised. 'There's cake for afters.'

Roland Young, as advertised, was without peer in *Blind Adventure* at the Cosy. Clive and Mary sat in the warm fug with fingers entwined. They were together, at the flicks on Saturday night, eating Jaffas and smiling at each other occasionally in the dark. Mary jumped slightly, then moved Clive's hand from her thigh, her eyes straight ahead on Roland Young in his unusual role of cat-burglar. The rejected hand lay in his lap, extra and unneeded as a spare limb.

'Next Saturday,' she said as they rode home against the head wind, 'it's *His Grace Gives Notice*. I'd like to see that.' He could see the gleam of her teeth beneath a street light. 'It's all about a duke pretending to be a footman.' She paused. 'And it's the Show soon.'

So it was all right then. She was happy to go out with him, to progress from biking home, to Saturday flicks, to going to the Annual Show together. 'Will you marry me?' he gasped.

She stopped pedalling. 'What?'

He braked in the middle of the road. 'Marry me.'

She stopped, adjusted her headlamp. 'Come in when we get home.'

'The thing is, Clive,' she said, handing him milky tea in an octagonal green cup. 'The thing is . . .' He felt cold; there didn't seem to be a heater. Bare scrim hung on the walls in patches where the wallpaper had peeled off. He lit a cigarette. No ashtray either.

Mary sat on a large cushion at his feet, her back to the empty grate. She leant forward, trying to explain, to make him see. To understand without pain. 'You're different,' she said.

Despair, familiar-since-childhood misery, clenched his gut. 'How?'

Her hair was loose around her shoulders, her eyes wide, begging him not to mind. 'It's not that I don't like you.' She paused, licked her lips. 'It's all right, going out and that. The Show even. But . . .'

He ground his cigarette out on the saucer. 'I'm not a pansy, if that's what you mean.'

She blushed scarlet. 'Oh, no. No! I didn't mean . . .'

'Or a mother's boy. You needn't think that. If you want to know . . . I hate her.' He paused panting. 'Hate her,' he gasped.

'Don't,' she whispered.

He wiped one sweating hand beneath an orange sateen cushion on the ancient sofa. She was so little, so gallant, with her no-hoper father and her Mrs Earnshaws and their bloody wool georgettes. 'I'll look after you,' said Clive.

'I've looked after myself since Mum died when I was ten.'

He leant back, reaching in the pocket of his grey flannels for his smokes. 'You'll have to marry someone,' he said.

Her head lifted. 'Why?'

'Well, because.' He was begging now, his hands clenched. 'So why not me?'

115

'No,' said Mary. 'I'm sorry, but no, no.'

'I'll wait.'

'No!'

She refused to see him, to answer the telephone. She ran for cover when he appeared.

He begged her, beseeched, mowed her lawns, bought her presents she tried to return; a pink quilted nightdress case with 'Nightie' stitched in blue; things for her glory box which made her weep; an organdie throwover, embroidered hankies, a golden toilet mirror and a salt and pepper set of red-nosed gnomes.

He hung around, persisted, would not go away. How could he possibly go away?

Ken Bates appeared at the china counter. He picked up a jam jar with a china strawberry on the lid, put it down again. 'Where's Miss Kirten?'

'Lunch.'

'I want a word with you, Clive. I'll make it quick. If you don't stop hanging around Mary Boyle I'll knock your block off.' His voice dropped. 'No flannel, I mean it. And it's a criminal offence. I'll put the cops on to you. Get it?'

Clive's hands clutched the counter. 'Offence?' he gasped.

'Like I said. Harassment.'

'But I love her.'

Ken Bates smiled his wide smile. His eyes crinkled. 'You, Clivey?' He shook his head sadly. 'What would Mum say?'

Clive snatched the jam jar, flung it at the tanned laughing face. It crashed to pieces, blood spurted, the strawberry rolled across the counter. 'Get out,' he screamed. 'Get out, y' sod!'

Mr Ken Bates, the popular manager of the grocery department at the Farmers' Co-op, has been selected for higher management training at Head Office, Wellington. Mr Bates and his family will leave the district next week.

'We'll be sad to leave our good friends here,' laughed Mr Bates, 'but promotion's promotion.'

She stood beside him at the bike racks.

'Hullo, Clive,' she said.

He swung around in astonishment, the chain of his padlock clanging. 'Mary?' She looked terrible. Ugly, almost. There was something wrong with her. Something had gone wrong.

'Are you all right?'

'Of course. Why shouldn't I be all right?'

'Yes, but . . .' Her eyes were black holes, pee holes in the snow. Ken Bates had said that, not about her, not about Mary at all. Someone else entirely. Clive was breathing hard. 'You look . . . you look sad.'

'Sad?' She ducked her head. 'Why would I be sad?'

'I don't know,' he muttered miserably.

She smiled up at him, put out her hand. 'Perhaps I'd cheer up if you'd bike me home.'

He stared, felt the tears in his eyes. 'OK,' he said. 'OK.'

The church was tastefully decorated by friends of the bride in belladonna lilies and lycopodium for the marriage of Mr Clive Harper to Miss Mary Boyle last Saturday.

The bride was beautifully gowned in white satin cut on classical lines, the yoke being trimmed with hand-made leaves and orange blossom. The bride made a charming picture as she entered the church on the arm of Dr York, a family friend. There was no train.

The bride was attended by her cousin, Miss Hazel Neltey, dressed in pale pink frilled organdie, with large organdie hat trimmed with deeper pink flowers. Frilled organdie gloves were worn and she carried a shower bouquet of pink carnations, dahlias and belladonna lilies and wore a rose quartz necklace, the gift of the bridegroom.

The reception was held at the Cornwall Park Tearooms. The bridegroom's mother, Mrs Harper Snr, acted as hostess. She wore brown figured crepe de chine and a brown hat and carried a bouquet of dahlias and carnations to tone.

The bride's going-away outfit was a cinnamon-brown suit with hat, shoes and gloves to tone. The honeymoon will be spent in Nelson. The couple's future home will be in Hastings.

They lay awake in the dark, rigid, scarcely able to breathe. Clive held her hand. 'It'll be all right,' he said finally. 'You know . . . later.'

Mary's hand moved in his. 'Yes.'

'You'll be tired,' he said hopelessly. He rolled towards her. 'Mary?'

'Yes?'

'It's probably that thing.'

'The frenchie?'

He lay still, startled by her knowledge.

'Why did you use it?' she whispered.

'Well. I mean we don't want a baby straight off, do you?'

She flung herself at him in the dark. 'Yes. Yes. I do.'

'Well, then, I'll just . . .'

She was sobbing; fierce, gulping angry sobs. 'No. No. No.'

He held her in his arms. 'Don't cry, don't cry. We've got plenty of time.'

'Yes,' she gasped.

'I love you.'

'I know,' she said. Her hand touched his hair. 'I know.'

He flung himself to his side of the bed, one hand groping for his smokes and matches.

Mrs Harper telephoned Dr York to tell him, her voice calm, almost brusque. She had always told Clive about smoking in bed. She'd told him and told him and told him.

Dr York spent a sleepless night, his eyes open as he waited for the morning newspaper. He spread it flat on the scrubbed-pine table in the kitchen and he read each word of the report with slow care. There was little detail.

Honeymoon Tragedy. Local Bride Dies.

A popular local bride and seamstress, Mrs Clive Harper (née Boyle), died in a hotel fire in Nelson last night. Mrs Harper and her husband were honeymooning in the South Island after their marriage in Hastings last week.

The fire is understood to have started in the bridal suite. Mr Harper, who was found unconscious in the corridor, is under sedation. Other guests were unharmed, but the hotel was extensively damaged.

A spokesman from the Fire Brigade said that rescue operations had been hampered by a strong wind.

Funeral details for Mrs Harper will be published in the Obituary Column of the Clarion *at a later date.*

Dr York put his head in his hands.

All right. So what would you have done? . . . Told him?

119

What good would that have done? He paused. And if you've any decency at all, make sure there's no post-mortem.

Mrs York appeared at the doorway. She stared at her husband's grief. He looked so old, so cold. She put her arms around his shoulders, kissed his bald head.

'There's no point in being morbid, George,' she said. 'That won't help anyone.'

Dr York moved his head slowly from side to side.

'Poor Clive,' he said. 'Poor, poor Clive.'

'Clive's all right,' snapped Mrs York. 'What about that poor child! What about Mary?'

'Oh yes.' Dr York's hand shook as he adjusted his glasses. 'Yes.' His head moved again. He raised myopic eyes to the white sky beyond the kitchen window, the bare branches. 'But poor Clive.'

So Lovely of Them

George had always been sure of himself, had known he was right, had made quick decisions and stuck by them. How else could he have been so successful, have had his own factory at thirty, made his first take-over at thirty-nine. A self-made man and proud of it, as who would not be. A good boss, they said on the factory floor, tough but fair. You knew where you were with him.

Except, thought Mavis, slipping out of striped cotton in the motel bedroom after lunch, that you didn't. Not in the home you didn't. Not in the home at all, and never had, and getting worse day by day in front of your very eyes.

It was understandable, of course, now he was retired. Quite understandable. One minute you were saying unto this man Go and he goeth and unto this man Come and he cometh and then overnight you're rattling around the house with a wife of thirty-five years and not another soul now Tom had gone to Melbourne. It was probably just that he was bored. No coming, no going, just Mavis to put through the hoops of punctuality, tidiness (lack of), powers of concentration (failing). Memory, he told her, is mind over matter. Muddle, he said, is trouble.

Mavis shook her head in quick dismissal. Such thoughts

121

are not for weddings and she was glad they had come to Tony's. Her favourite nephew after all, and Fielding such a pretty little place in the spring. All blossom, catkins and lambs, it had been a lovely drive up. And fun being part of it, staying in the same motel with the bridegroom and the rest of the wedding party. 'Are you part of the Wedding Party?' the lady had asked. 'The rest of the Wedding Party are at the rehearsal.' Things like that. It made you feel welcome even if you had given the happy couple their third travelling iron which had seemed such such a good idea at the time with them both going off for three years. He and Betsy had been sweet about it. Still . . .

The wedding was timed for three at the Presbyterian church. Mavis and her sister Bet had agreed they would have time to put their feet up before starting.

Not that they got much rest. The bridesmaids ran along narrow corridors shrieking with laughter and looking for the laundry and a quick press. Someone had mislaid a belt, two cousins had swapped hats, the groomsmen were yahooing around the place trying to find the Going Away Car so they could mess it up with confetti and stuff like they do at country weddings, though less often now.

Just as she was nodding off George appeared from the en suite clutching the *Dominion*. You either do or you don't read the newspaper in the toilet and she had given up on the whole thing long ago. But it seemed worse somehow when it was right next door, the cistern rushing and clanking and all so immediate.

He dropped the paper on the candlewick bedspread. 'I'm going to do a recce,' he said.

She edged away from the thing. 'What for?'

'The church. We don't know where the church is.'

122

'Bet and Doug'll tell us.'

'Time spent on reconnaisance,' said George, 'is never wasted.'

She knew this. She also knew that a good man leads from the front and that if you have time to spare you should go by air. Mavis smoothed flesh-pink nylon over her front with one hand and closed her eyes. Mad, she thought dreamily. Quite mad.

He arrived back in good spirits having found the Presbyterian church. It would be no problem. All would be well.

Mavis, now dressed and preoccupied with her hat, made small encouraging noises. She had made an effort with the hat, had gone to Mercer's in her blue, had sought advice from the young woman with the teeth who had suggested eau de nil to tone. The hat now sat on her head like a pale green meringue, its white silk daisies wreathed in tulle. It refused to settle, to become part of her. It remained perched, disparate as a seagull on the bronze head of Sir Keith Holyoake's statue in Molesworth Street.

Mavis turned for help. 'How do I look?' she asked.

George glanced at his watch. 'Gone in fifteen minutes.'

'Fifteen!'

'It's right the other side of town.'

'But this is *Fielding*.'

'I've just been there, haven't I? And we want a good park.'

Why, she wondered, remembering not to panic at the unexpectedly shortened time, did they need a *good* park? There would be a church, there would be room to park. Why a good one? In Fielding.

She moistened her lips, gave her image a small tentative

smile. The stranger's lips moved in response. The face looked tired, its normal pink now tinged with green beneath fluorescent light and tulle. There were strange bruised shadows beneath the eyes.

'Pull yourself together,' snapped Mavis at the defeated-looking thing. It knew as well as she did. It's simply a matter of doing the best you can with what's left.

'Coming, George?' she called.

George re-appeared. He was still a good-looking man, a well-dressed man at ease with himself and destiny. He glanced in the mirror, smoothed his hair. 'Don't *fuss*, woman,' he said. 'We've got plenty of time.'

They drove through Fielding in silence. Neat houses sat in rows surrounded by well-mown lawns. Roses were in full bloom, an occasional rampant climber waved high in triumph. Sharp green foliage covered old trees, the roads were wide and empty.

'It seems a long way,' she said.

'I told you.'

'Yes.'

They pulled into the churchyard, parked the car beside the small white church and sat silent.

'There's nobody here,' said Mavis finally.

He checked his watch. 'There should be.'

'Well there isn't.'

George lifted his eyes to the pointed wooden spire. 'They'll come.'

Mavis leaped from the car.

'Where are you going?' he cried.

She clutched the iron ring of the church door and rattled. The door was locked. She beat on its wooden

panels with both fists, a supplicant begging for sanctuary.
There was no reply. The air was warm and heavy, the
silence unbroken except for the soaring song of a skylark
and the frustrated bellow of a nearby bull.

She ran down the steps, flung open George's door.

'It's the wrong church!'

He waved a hand at a nearby hoarding. FIELDING
PRESBYTERIAN CHURCH, it said. The Minister was
named, the times of service, the extramural activities. All
were welcome.

'You wanted a Presbyterian church. You've got one.'

If only the bull would shut up. 'There – is – no – one –
here. There must be two.'

'In Fielding?'

There had been a time a thousand years ago when she
had found that slow smile endearing. Mavis could feel her
heart, hear her deep rickety breaths. 'It's a quarter to
three,' she shouted. 'And there is *no one here*.'

He lay back in the seat and closed his eyes.

If only Tom were here. He could deal with his father,
has always been able to from an early age. Had refused to
be reduced to pulp by imbecility, to be bullied by irrational
behaviour. But Tom, good staunch Tom was doing very
well in the bank in South Yarra and he and Sue were
looking forward to seeing them both next month, in fact
they could hardly wait.

Mavis gave a small strangled noise and spoke to closed
eyelids. 'I'm going to find the other one,' she said.

'Do that.'

She slammed the door and set off, wobbling across small
stones in her new navy courts, sweat dampening her face,
her hat slipping. Rage impelled her, marched her swollen

125

feet forward and carried her onto the grass verge beyond the church gates.

'Excuse me,' she said to a young man standing thoughtfully beside a large freshly dug hole in the middle of his front lawn. Foundations? Sewage? An ornamental concrete pond with bridge? All, all were irrelevant.

'Can you tell me where the *other* Presbyterian church is?' asked Mavis. She gave a light laugh. It could happen to anyone, she intimated, part of the human condition, here a church, there a church, you can never be sure till you ask.

He pointed. 'First right, first left, and right again.' He glanced at her feet. 'It's quite a long way.'

'Thank you.' She gave a quick backwards movement of her head. 'My husband will be coming soon.'

The young man lifted a hand in salute. 'Go for it,' he said and resumed his silent contemplation of the hole in the ground.

They had had a wonderful time in Melbourne with Tom and Sue fussing over them, such a welcome and so kind. And Jamie a real little boy now with that haircut, and fancy him remembering. And their idea, their lovely idea had left Mavis, and George as well, quite speechless. It was so kind, so generous, so, so well . . . loving.

A booking had been made for them both for a night in a first-class hotel on the Bellalarine Peninusula; dinner, bed and breakfast for two and see a bit of the country at the same time. An early Christmas present, all paid in advance. They would get the train from Spencer Street, the bus from Geelong. They would have a ball.

And so they had so far. George was good at journeys. Things which involved timetables and keys, departures and arrivals pleased him, especially when the transport was punctual. Mussolini, he told her, had made the Italian trains run on time. Mavis nodded. 'I read somewhere,' she said, 'that the bodies of Mussolini and his mistress. Carla someone . . .'

'Petacci.'

'Yes, well . . . they were shown to the crowds hanging upside down. Someone had tied her skirt around her knees, but even so . . . The misery he'd inflicted, the misery of course, for so long. But upside *down*. Like being buried standing on your head. Not that it would matter, I can see that, but the idea appals me.' She stared over flat dry plains, shaking her head at tin sheds and sparse scrubby bush. 'Appals,' she murmured.

'You're all over the place as usual. I'm talking about *trains*.'

'Yes.'

They clambered from the train at Geelong. Tom had given them directions. They read them carefully. 'Get bus to Queenscliff at Station.'

George strode off purposefully. Mavis followed. It was very hot. Thirty-five degrees the man had said, and more to come. Trickles of sweat ran down the back of her knees, slid between her breasts as she headed towards the bus park to the right. George strode straight ahead. Mavis put her grip down. 'The bus park,' she said, 'is over here.'

'It's this way.'

Gentle Jesus, meek and mild. 'George,' said Mavis, 'I can see the *signs*.'

'I'm going this way,' he said and did so.

Mavis stood watching his straight back, his decisive stride into nowhere. He stopped beneath a wattle tree and

127

a sign for a local bus stop. Mavis picked up her grip and walked over to the sign labelled *Queenscliff*. The next bus was due, she read, at twelve-fifteen.

Primary school children passed, hatted like miniature French Foreign Legionnaires. Old women toiled by in tied-on straws. A shop window advertised cotton jamas with racing cars. Perhaps she could get a pair for Jamie. No, no time.

She felt curiously empty, devoid of any emotion, either of empathy or distaste. A hot hatless old woman waiting for a bus. She looked over at George standing upright and resolute in the wrong place. She was not concerned. No sweat, as Tom might inaccurately have said. The Queens-cliff bus would arrive, she would climb in. George would abandon his heroic stand on the wrong deck and come to join her. Not a word would be said.

Mavis stared straight ahead. At the far end of the square two young abseiling workmen were engaged in mounting a giant roll of white plastic sheeting to the blank wall of a multi-storeyed building. They pranced about its vertical face, their rubber-shod toes bobbing and leaping on French Vanilla stucco, their harnesses suspended from steel ropes far above. Their neat rear ends were safely strapped, their hands free. As she watched, each one swung to an opposite side to cut the bindings of the roll.

Its descent was dramatic, instantaneous and complete. Its message was proclaimed in Christmas Tree shape, in letters of foot-high green.

FED FAX
Wish all their customers
a VERY HAPPY CHRISTMAS
and a PROSPEROUS NEW YEAR
YOUR FUTURE LIES WITH FED FAX
THRU
1998
1999
2000
and the Rest
of the
MILLENNIUM

The word made visible, the mission statement confirmed. There was a sense of proclamation, of Hear Ye, Hear Ye, flapping gently but securely at the end of the square. The two young men descended at speed, unbuckled, and disappeared in a flash.

Mavis stared at it.

The news brought her no redress. The rest of the millennium. Dear God, what a thought. A thousand ages in thy sight may well be like an evening gone. I understand that, I'm not disputing it for a moment. But not for me, God. Please, Sweet Christ, not for me. Her eyes filled, tears welled over, unbidden and inevitable as overflow.

Half blinded, sweating, Mavis mounted the steps as the bus arrived. There was no hand free to wipe her eyes and anyway what did it matter. Look at the rest of them; the fat angry driver, the little woman with the tic, the old man with his strange basket. Where on earth did they think they were going and what in Heaven's name did it matter if there were tears or no tears.

George strode across the parade ground. He climbed the steps and called to her. 'Have you paid?'

'Not for you.'

The driver took his money with a wink.

George stowed his bag and sat beside her in silence. She turned her sodden face to the window and mopped. Be still, be still.

After some time she faced the front, her expression, she hoped, non-judgmental, but how could you know.

His voice was startled. Mavis was weeping. Mavis never cried, never, let alone *wept*. 'What the hell's wrong now?'

'Wrong how?'

'Why are you crying, for God's sake? We haven't even got there yet.'

'Oh.' Mavis drew a deep breath. She was now crying loudly, uncontrollably as a small child. Tears sprang from her eyes to splash unheeded down her face. 'That's just it,' she gasped. 'I was thinking,' she hiccupped, 'thinking about Tom and Sue. It's so lovely, so lovely of them. So generous,' she bawled, mopping and banging about with a screwed-up rag with polka dots. 'So lovely.'

George drew a clean white handkerchief from his trouser pocket and handed it to her in silence.

Gasping, sobbing, clutching at straws, she took it.

He put a large freckled hand on the knee beside him and squeezed slightly.

'You'll be better when we get there,' he said.